Blue Death

■ ■ ■

#7 in the Edgar Award-winning
Dan Fortune mystery series

Dennis Lynds

Originally published under the pseudonym Michael Collins

To Anne and Larry, in hope

Acclaim for Dennis Lynds & His Novels

"A gripping story." – *The Charlotte Observer*

"Action and intrigue are nicely mixed." – *Publishers Weekly*

"A novelist of power and quality … one of the major imaginative creators in the crime field." – Ross Macdonald

"Like Ross Macdonald, Michael Collins can write vivid prose and dialogue *and* plot a mystery." – *Ellery Queen Mystery Magazine*

"First-class … suspenseful, character-rich, and absorbing." – *Kirkus Reviews*

"Some of the rawest, most unencumbered mystery writing extant in the genre." – *American Library Association*

"Tough, believable." – *San Francisco Examiner*

"Finely honed suspense." – *New York Times*

"[Lynds's books are] filled with as much closely observed incident and detail as John O'Hara short stories." – *Wall Street Journal*

"[He] carries on the Hammett-Chandler-Macdonald tradition with skill and finesse." – *Washington Post Book World*

"...combines superb characters and excellent plotting." – *ALA Booklist*

"... powerful writing." – *Library Journal*

"... engrossing and empathic." – *New York Daily News*

"... hot mystery writer whose novels have reached mainstream status. ..." – *San Diego Reporter*

"Collins is the Costa-Gavras of the PI world ... we might also call him the Captain Kirk of PI writers, boldly taking the genre where no colleague has gone before – and doing it so passionately that we can't help but sign on for the quest with him." – literary critic Francis M. Nevins, Jr.

"Lynds is a major contributor to the form, even a redefiner of it; whether or not he is ever given his just due, he should take satisfaction from the fact that he has written mystery novels of genuine distinction." – literary critic Richard Carpenter

Dan Fortune series, by Dennis Lynds, originally published under the pseudonym Michael Collins

Act of Fear, 1967
The Brass Rainbow, 1969
Night of the Toads, 1970
Walk a Black Wind, 1971
Shadow of a Tiger, 1972
The Silent Scream, 1973
Blue Death, 1975
The Blood-Red Dream, 1976
The Nightrunners, 1978
The Slasher, 1980
Freak, 1983
Minnesota Strip, 1987
Red Rosa, 1988
A Dangerous Job, 1989
Chasing Eights, 1990
The Irishman's Horse, 1991
Cassandra In Red, 1992

Paul Shaw series, by Dennis Lynds, originally published under the pseudonym Mark Sadler

The Falling Man, 1970
Here to Die, 1971
Mirror Image, 1972
Circle of Fire, 1973
Touch of Death, 1981
Deadly Innocents, 1986

Kane Jackson series, by Dennis Lynds, originally published under the pseudonym William Arden

A Dark Power, 1968
Deal in Violence, 1969
The Goliath Scheme, 1971

Die to a Distant Drum, 1972
Deadly Legacy, 1973

Buena Costa County series, by Dennis Lynds, originally published under the pseudonym John Crowe
Another Way to Die, 1972
A Touch of Darkness, 1972
Bloodwater, 1974
Crooked Shadows, 1975
When They Kill Your Wife, 1977
Close to Death, 1979

George Malcolm, private detective, by Dennis Lynds, originally published under the pseudonym Carl Dekker
Woman in Marble, 1973

Langford ("Ford") Morgan, ex-soldier, ex-CIA, ex-roustabout, by Dennis Lynds, originally published under the pseudonym Michael Collins
The Cadillac Cowboy, 1995

Other of his works include science fiction novels, literary novels, mystery short stories, literary short stories, short story anthologies, and poetry.

Table of Contents

1

Black-haired, exotic, with large almond eyes, Leslie Ajemian sat in my office, nervous in a worn green dress, and I thought of the difference between what's supposed to be and what is.

"Dan the Pirate." She smiled on only half her face. "You haven't changed."

"You have," I said.

Three years since I'd seen her—maybe four. The green dress probably new then. Now it was shabby. Neat, but cleaned too many times, tight over her full breasts. I remembered those breasts—firm and pale brown like the rest of her body. The body she'd made her living with belly-dancing fantasies for drunks in the Third Street club where Marty had worked.

"I tried hard," she said. "Decided I'd rather have sold myself straight than gone on being live bait for cut booze."

She'd learned the difference between a dream of dancing and the reality of that leering club. What was supposed to be, and what was. (That's one of the things I talk to myself about in dark doorways: the difference between a bank's TV promises and getting a real loan; between the words on the Statue of Liberty and a nation that needed cheap labor. I solve the world's problems in those solitary doorways. Sure I do.)

"I was never going to be good enough to get out of that club, a chorus line at best," she said. "I wanted more, something real." She lit a cigarette. "You heard I got married?"

"I heard."

"A good man, Dan. He works hard."

When she called me, I'd known it wasn't for old times. But she hadn't said why she wanted a detective. Now I knew—her husband or her marriage. They weren't always the same.

"He's something more?" I said. "Something real?"

I heard the sneer in my voice. Too hot for a September morning, and I had my own trouble. They were going to tear my building down, and all at once I loved the grimy air shaft, the cracked ceiling and worn floor, the odd tenants who made a precarious living as middlemen in thin businesses, as dealers in dusty objects no one had ever heard of. Leslie saw the look on my face, and misinterpreted it.

"I haven't seen Marty in a while, Dan," she said.

Martine Adair, who'd wanted more, too. More than she could have with a one-armed detective in a one-window office in Chelsea. Water under the bridge, like my lost arm. Except I lost the arm thirty years ago, and I still think about it. Maybe Leslie hadn't misinterpreted me.

"We went different ways after she married that director," Leslie said. "She still wants show business."

"Isn't your husband helping your career? You want me to help you dump him? So you can find a director, too?"

She got up and started for the door.

What the hell was I doing? So they were tearing down my building, and she'd made me think of Marty. Two things surer than taxes, if not death, were that if you want a dynamic woman you take a risk, and if you live in New York your building's going to be torn down sooner or later.

"Leslie?" I said. "Sorry. Sit down."

She stopped at the door, like an arrow on a taut string. Then she sat down again. Whatever she wanted me to do was more urgent than her anger or her pride.

She lit another cigarette. "Maybe it's nothing, Dan, but Jake feels so helpless, and so do I. It's beating him."

"Your husband?"

"Jake Carter," she said. "Born and raised over in Newark, just like me. Leslie Carter, that's my name now."

She smoked. "You know how I lived at that club—a new man a week, vodka for breakfast at three P.M. Furs, dresses, and gaudy promises that never would happen." Her dark, almost Arab eyes fixed on my face. "Jake's not sharp or educated. He never had a decent job, had his trouble in Newark gangs. But he wants more, too. We run a parking business—one small garage, three open lots. We have an apartment in the Village, some money for fun, and don't owe anyone. Solid citizens."

"Then what's beating your husband?"

She smoothed her worn dress. "It's a cutthroat business, Dan. Every time a building comes down, ten garage operators try to lease the empty lot. Jake runs our lots for all they can handle, double car racks every inch he can fit them. But we need all three to make a living. Our best lot is on Eighth Avenue near Twenty-ninth. The lease is up; Jake went to renew."

She stubbed out her cigarette, lit another. "He's got the money in his hand, but he can't find anyone to take it!"

"The owner won't renew? You don't have an option?"

"Sure we have an option, and we don't know if they'll renew or not! Jake can't find anyone to talk to!"

"Who's the owner?"

"International Metals and Refining Corporation."

"They're a big company. Their own building, right?"

"IMR Center. Thirty stories, all glass, and right next to our lot. Their lobby rug costs more than the lot. We leased it a year ago from their real estate manager, an assistant VP named Berger. Now Jake can't even get near him!"

"He doesn't know any reason?"

"He says he gets passed from office to office. They don't throw him out; they just send him in circles!"

"Could this Berger want something? A shakedown?"

"A big company like IMR?"

"Big companies hire small men," I said. I studied her face. "Could Jake have done anything?"

"No!"

Too quick, too sharp. As if she had a doubt. A doubt she wanted to deny, but couldn't. Her dream was a place in life to be proud of, something solid to grow old with. I didn't know what Jake Carter's dream was. She'd told me, but I didn't know.

"You said Jake had troubles in Newark," I said. "What?"

"Street gangs, and later those vigilantes of Senator Imperiale. Fights, riots, robberies. He was only arrested once."

I waited, but she was silent. "What for, Leslie?"

Reluctant. "The kid vigilantes got money from shopkeepers to fight the blacks. Political funds."

"Extortion," I said.

"He wasn't even charged! It was a long time ago now."

"What do you want me to do, Leslie?"

"You know how to find people, reach them, talk to them."

"I've got no influence at IMR or anywhere else."

"You're the only detective I know. A friend."

"And cheap," I said, smiled.

She didn't smile. "Dan, find out what's wrong."

"All right. Where's Jake now?"

"At the IMR lot. Do I pay you? Is fifty okay?"

After she left, I sat folding the bills in the hot office. Not enough for a real job, but, then, I wasn't sure there was a job. I slipped my tie into my pocket. On the street, I looked up at my building. A sagging Chelsea office building where the "businessmen" slept in the office half the time to save double rent. But Chelsea was changing again now.

I saw it as I walked to Eighth Avenue and turned north. In the new and renovated apartments of one-room studios at heavy rents, in the small restaurants. The young were moving in. I like the young, but I liked my Chelsea, too. Where my father had changed Fortunowski to Fortune, where I'd been born—if I had gone away too long and too far to really belong now. Only half at home, but half a home was better than none, and no one wants to be the victim of change.

The Carter parking lot on Eighth was full, bordered on the south by fenced yards of slum brownstones, on the north by the towering glass-and-steel of IMR Center. The office was a shack near a yard fence. As I neared it, two ragged boys burst out of an opening in the fence and ran past me. I watched them until they vanished into the crowd on the avenue, turned, and the three men were on top of me!

A face like a skeleton. A swarthy face. A bearded face.

A long club in a bony hand hitting down.

I fell among the cars, tried to fend off the club, but my one arm was against me.

The three faces swarmed like giant insects in the sun.

2

"You all right?"

He bent over me. A beard and vague blue eyes. His beard was trimmed and neat, like the beard of a professor I had in one of the colleges where I'd studied a lot without learning anything I could sell.

"I guess the old man must be crazy," he said. "This city."

I sat up. My head hurt, but not much. I had no feeling of time passing, the cars still filled the lot. Momentarily stunned. I stood up. The bearded man held out a hand to help me, staring as if only now aware that I was missing an arm. His other hand held to a car. I smelled the martinis.

"Some kids bothered his dogs," he said, thought about it. "Guess he thought you were with them. Jake stopped him."

His pale eyes blinked at me as if he had more to say but couldn't remember what. It was early for martinis, even in New York, and he didn't look like a martini type. In his early forties, average size. With the beard, medium long hair, bell trousers, low boots, and a wrinkled blue blazer, he looked like a semi-hippie in town on reluctant business.

"My car's here," he remembered. "Jake and I had drinks."

On my feet now, I looked for the other two. They were near the office shack. The one who had to be Jake Carter was glaring at the skeletonlike old man.

"What the hell you doing, Ben?" Carter was saying.

"Yellin' in my ear all day, botherin' the dogs, makin' them bark. Dirty little punks," the old man said.

His voice was thin and flat like some narrow Yankee farmer. At least seventy-five, bone-thin and leaning on the cane he'd hit me with. The bearded man shook his head beside me.

"They're giving Jake a lousy deal," he said.

"They are?" I said. "Why?"

"Walk away," he said. "That's the answer."

Taking his own advice, he walked off toward the office shack. I followed as far as Jake Carter and the old man.

"Christ," Carter swore. "They feed the dogs, walk them."

"I got a right to protect my property," the old man said. "They got no right to trespass, excite the dogs."

"But they can feed them, walk them, buy the food?"

"I ain't *told* no one to feed 'em. You remember."

"You're a bastard, Ben," Jake Carter said. "A mean old bastard! Get off my lot."

The old man turned so sharply he nearly fell. He limped away. Jake Carter's nostrils flared with anger.

"Six mongrels in a wire pen," he said. "Never washes them or cleans the pen. If the kids didn't do it all, they'd die."

The old man stopped at the opening in the fence. His old face was pinched, his voice bitter:

"My mother was legal married. You got no call sayin' lies about me 'n my family. Ain't even your own lot."

He hobbled into a brownstone. Beside me, Jake Carter began to shiver with repressed fury. A broad-faced, swarthy man in his thirties, about my height—five-feet-ten. In a garage uniform he was a good thirty pounds heavier than my one hundred and sixty, with a plain, rugged face. He hadn't shaved today, and his hands clenched and unclenched at his sides.

"The dirty, stinking old son-of-a-bitch," he said.

He took deep breaths and looked all around as if his anger was for more than one old man, for the whole city.

"Jake?" I said. "I'm Dan Fortune. Leslie sent me to see you. I'm a private detective and an old friend."

He walked away into the office shack, slammed the door.

I went after him slowly. Inside the shack he was already seated at a desk working on papers. The bearded man with the vague blue eyes and martini breath sat in a dim corner.

"You don't want any help?" I said to Carter. "Leslie says you're getting a runaround, can't give your money away."

"I'll handle it, Fortune."

The bearded man shook his head. "A man alone can't handle it. They handle it. Make you rich, make you poor."

Carter said, "You want your car, Mr. Pike?"

"Car?" He had that immobility of midday drinkers, detached from time. "No, no car. How about some more drinks? And the name is Carl."

"I've got work," Jake Carter said.

"At IMR?" I said. "Why won't they renew your lease?"

"Busy people, right? All on vacation, down at the beach."

The bearded man said, "Sea, mountains, sleep with the sound of waves." His blue eyes focused. "How far is the sea?"

"River's a few blocks west," Carter said. "Want your car?"

The bearded man stood up and walked out. I watched him turn west toward the river, walking fast.

"I get all the nuts," Jake Carter said.

"You don't know him?"

Carter shook his head. "Met him this morning waiting around at IMR. Mr. Carl Pike—call me Carl. Latched onto me, bought me a couple of beers."

"If he works at IMR, maybe he can help."

"I don't need any help."

"Leslie thinks you do."

He picked up his pen, began to work on his papers.

"What doesn't Leslie know?" I said. "Is it a shakedown? Berger wants money? Is one of your competitors bribing him?"

He went on working on his papers.

"If it's anything like that," I said, "don't try to handle it alone, do something stupid."

"You drumming up business?"

"All right. Hire a lawyer then. See the police."

He worked. "I'll take care of it."

"Or," I said, "is it the other way? Maybe you tried some game, got in trouble with IMR?"

"So she told you about Newark?" He sat back. "I don't know you, I don't owe you answers, but you hear this—Newark is long gone. I saw that our kid gangs was no different from the black kid gangs—punks, junior Mafia. The vigilantes were bigots and boss dagos who wanted to stay in power. I wanted a future. I work hard, I make a living, I've got a future. Okay?"

"You've got a worried wife, too, and you're wound up tight. You leaned on that old man pretty hard."

"He had it coming, the old bastard!"

"Look, let me try to—"

"Damn her, this is my business! Get out of here!"

There was a rack of wrenches on the wall behind him. He swung violently in his chair, grabbed one, and raised it. We faced each other a moment. Then I walked out.

In the hot sun I took a breath. He owed me nothing, I owed him nothing. IMR was a big company too busy to see a small man. Or was there more? Something that could hurt Leslie? I could hear the doubt in her voice there in my office. Half aware that Jake was involved in something, or only afraid he was?

I didn't owe him, but I owed her. For old times and fifty dollars. How much did I owe her for fifty? At least a try for a simple answer? That much I owed her, unless she was using me for her own reasons. It had been done before.

Walter Berger's office was on the twenty-eighth floor of IMR Center, medium-sized, with two windows, and his secretary was sorry he wasn't in it. He was very busy this week.

"Fill out a form, Mr. Berger will call you," she said.

"If I don't fill out a form, who'll talk to me now?"

"Miss Montrose is in charge of this division."

Ruth Montrose, vice president, had a large center office a floor higher and with four windows. Her secretary had heard that Mr. Berger was on vacation, she was *very* sorry, but:

"I'm afraid Veep Montrose is uptown. If you'll fill out this form, I'll be happy to make an appointment."

It was the same form. "Is there someone higher up?"

"Of course," she smiled. "Mr. Weaver, executive vice president. Next floor up."

Mr. Franklin Weaver had a large corner office on the top floor. I don't know how many windows it had; I didn't even reach his secretary. A floor receptionist stopped me.

"Miss Hahn's in a meeting. If you'll fill out a form, I'm sure she'll find a place in Mr. Weaver's schedule soon."

"You have a president?"

"Only by strict appointment. If you'll—"

"I know, fill out a form. Look, it's a small real estate deal, nothing big, but it can't wait."

"Mr. Berger handles real estate," she said, smiled nicely. "Three floors down, but I heard he's working at home."

"I'll go down and fill out a form," I said.

I went down. Berger's secretary didn't give out home telephone numbers, but perhaps I could see Mr. Vasto.

"Can he renew the lease on your lot next door?" I asked.

"No. Mr. Berger handles that himself."

"Then who needs Mr. Vasto?" I said.

I wondered about a department head who handled routine details himself. Maybe Berger was busy, but why couldn't an assistant handle a two-bit lease? I went back up to Ruth Montrose's office. Her assistant was in Boston. Mr. Weaver, and Miss Hahn, stayed invisible. Berger's secretary still smiled.

I felt like some Eastern European trying to get a passport. This was an American runaround—smiles, politeness, forms, and public relations—but the result was the same. I wondered if there was anyone behind all those doors, or if there were only secretaries outside empty offices.

It was after three P.M. when I worked my way up to the top floor again. This time I slid by the receptionist into executive-VP Franklin Weaver's outer office. A woman was clearing her desk. A big girl with short black hair and a round face, wearing a navy blue dress with a white collar, working crisply.

"Miss Hahn?"

She looked up. Five-eleven, big-breasted, her face was mild and soft. Until she saw me. Her eyes flashed fiercely.

"No one announced—"

"I passed up the announcement. I want to see Weaver."

"*Mr.* Weaver is out! Now *you* get out. Right now. Out! Disturbing Mr. Weaver without—"

"If he's out, I'm not disturbing him," I said. "I'd like to disturb him a little, though. How do I get to do that?"

"Not by being sarcastic or impertinent!"

An educated girl for a secretary. But top executives pay well for that, expect independent work and fierce protection. I had the feeling that Miss Hahn delivered both.

"I'm sorry," I said. "It's just about a small lease—"

"Not Mr. Carter again? He's really annoying us, and I've told him that Mr. Berger handles that, Mr.—?"

"Dan Fortune," I said. "Mr. Berger seems to be a ghost."

"Oh, he's out sick; I forgot. But I'm sure—"

"Sick?" I said. "I've heard he's busy, on vacation, and working at home. Now you say sick. Just where is Berger?"

She was puzzled. "I know Mr. Weaver said he was ill."

"Maybe that's what Berger told Weaver," I said.

"I don't really know," she said, but she wondered.

"Maybe Weaver does. If not, maybe he should."

"He's very busy," she said. "It's a bad week."

"It's a worse week for Jake Carter. Mr. Weaver could probably cut a lot of red tape. Can I wait for him?"

"We close the office at three. I was just going home."

"Three P.M.? I thought Weaver was so busy?"

She bristled. Not as sophisticated as she tried to seem, or as cool. Young and loyal.

"I open the office at eight," she said hotly, "and he's here before I am! He has a chauffeur just so he can work on the way in. I leave at three, unless I'm needed, but he works past nine every night somewhere."

"A long day at his age," I agreed.

She laughed. "He's thirty-seven, Mr. Fortune."

When executive vice presidents are a lot younger than you, you feel old. I told myself Weaver was exceptional.

"Where does he do this work past nine?" I asked.

She hesitated, and her face softened. "Well, perhaps he won't mind. Perhaps he should be told about Mr. Berger."

"I appreciate it; Jake Carter needs that lot," I said. "Besides, I'm supposed to be a detective. I find people."

She laughed again, slung a heavy handbag over her shoulder, and walked out to the elevators ahead of me. A big girl, striding out with vigor.

On the avenue we got a taxi uptown. It dropped us across the street from a swank athletic club. The heat had melted the crowds into a slow-moving mass, and jammed the traffic. As I started to push our way across the street, I saw Jake Carter.

He was standing alone just up the street from the athletic club entrance. I pushed our way across, but when we got there, Carter was gone.

3

I looked up and down the crowded afternoon street, but Carter had vanished. In the frigid lobby of the athletic club, a uniformed attendant saw me and hurried up as if he expected trouble. Then he saw Miss Hahn, bowed us in. Mr. Weaver and his party were in the mezzanine lounge.

Half a flight up, the lounge was cool and hushed, but Weaver wasn't there. Miss Hahn approached two women seated at a table in a secluded corner. The older woman saw us:

"Yes, Hahn?"

She was small, in her forties, and wore a black shantung dress with a gold watch on the breast. A little plump, she had a small, oval face, and wore her straight brown hair chopped at the shoulders. There was a streak of gray in the brown hair.

"Isn't Mr. Weaver here, Miss Montrose?" Miss Hahn asked.

Ruth Montrose, IMR vice president, lit a long cigarette, let it dangle from a loose wrist. Disdainful, with the chopped-off hair and gray streak, it toughened her face.

"In the gym, Emily," she said. "For his mandatory workout. Mrs. Pike and I are just finishing our drinks."

I said, "Mrs. Carl Pike?"

"You know my husband?" the second woman said, looking at me and my empty sleeve.

She had a smooth, classical face. What was called "chaste beauty" in Victorian days. A Gibson girl without the long skirt. Instead, she wore a rich white blouse, a pale blue casual skirt, and a blue scarf at her throat. Exactly right for the day, and for her auburn hair. Almost haughty. Cool, yet somehow sensual, with intelligent eyes. Thirtyish.

"I ran into him earlier," I said. "A little drunk. Took a walk to the river."

"Did he?" she said.

Ruth Montrose said, "Who is this gentleman, Emily?"

"Mr. Fortune wants to ask about a lease on the empty lot next to IMR Center, Miss Montrose," Emily Hahn said. "He—"

"I don't advise it," Ruth Montrose said, eyed me over her cigarette. "Nugent just threw out one man who wanted to talk about that lease." She got up. "Carol?"

I said, "Maybe you can renew—"

"Come to the office properly," Ruth Montrose snapped.

She took Carol Pike's arm and left the lounge. I couldn't stop her here. Emily Hahn flushed angrily.

"I'm sorry. Miss Montrose can be arrogant. She's got a difficult job with both research and new construction. I'll get Tom Nugent to take a message in to Mr. Weaver."

She walked toward a small bar in one corner of the lounge. A man sat at one end. A giant. Sitting down, he was as tall as I was. At least two hundred and seventy pounds, at six-feet-eight or more he was almost slender when he stood to greet Emily Hahn. He had a stylish mustache, wore a dark blue suit on his massive shoulders.

"He's in the gym now, Emily," he said.

He moved with the confidence of his size, but his voice was careful as if correcting poor speech habits. A one-time football player, I guessed. Thirty-plus now, wearing horn-rimmed glasses and a serious manner.

"Would you take a message in, Tommy?" Emily Hahn said.

"What message?"

She told him. He shook his head. A man on duty, intense about it. Except for his size, he reminded me of a male secretary, a combination of assistant and old-fashioned batman.

"Mr. Weaver's too busy for that. I just had to throw out a guy asking about that lot," he said, apologetic, as if he hated to have to use physical action now, wanted a different success.

"Try, Tommy, all right?" Emily Hahn said. "It seems Mr. Berger can't be found, and the lease is almost up."

"I'll tell him," Nugent said.

He went through an unmarked door at the end of the lounge.

"I'll wait," I said to Emily Hahn. "You go on home."

She nodded and went. I waited. I waited two hours. Then I asked the gym attendant. Mr. Weaver and Mr. Nugent had left an hour ago. I didn't exist. That made me mad.

The tools of a detective are brains, work, luck and contacts, and if your contacts are really good, you can forget the other three. I got Franklin Weaver's home address from one of my best contacts—a credit-check company. His home addresses, he had two: in Connecticut, and on Park Avenue.

I had some dinner, so it was after seven when the taxi let me out at the building on Park. It had a doorman. I used my ring of keys on the service entrance, found the right elevator. It was self-service, served only one apartment on each floor. On Weaver's floor, a woman's voice spoke through a microphone.

"Mrs. Weaver?" I said. "I'm a private detective, Dan Fortune. Your husband told me to meet him here."

Silence behind the peephole in the heavy door.

"Here's my license." I held it up, took a chance. "You can call Miss Hahn if you want."

It worked; she opened the door. Secure people forget that two names are as easy to get as one. Inside, she walked into a vast living room. A rich apartment, but reserved, every piece a collector's item. Mrs. Weaver offered me a cigarette, let me light hers, and smiled politely.

"Sit down, Mr. Fortune. How do you know my husband?"

She was a big, soft woman in a red evening dress. Full-hipped but small-breasted, with a routine face and a finishing school voice. Money and family, a well-bred young matron. Over thirty, and looked it. Not good taste to be too beautiful, or to try to look younger. She was probably good on a horse, and had gone to the best schools. She used my name after hearing it once, and let me manipulate cigarette and lighter with my one hand without comment or trying to interfere.

"I do work for IMR," I said. "Industrial snooping."

"Really? At IMR?"

"It's the fashion."

"Yes," she nodded. "Would you like a drink? Coffee?"

"No, thanks."

She sat down; she had a guest. "This awful heat. At least Connecticut is cool for the children. You live in the city?"

"Yes, I'm lazy. Mr. Weaver must get up before seven."

She laughed. "Frank gets up at five. He plays tennis, swims, and takes the sauna before being driven in. It would kill me, but it must suit him; he's done quite well."

Executive vice president of an international corporation at thirty-seven was "doing quite well" to her. Everything's relative. Or did I detect a little bitterness?

"Not much time left for you," I said.

"I don't have much free time myself," she said quietly. "Two children, the house, the community, and the company. Frank has to entertain a great deal. I'm afraid I do a lot of shopping, you know? Clothes and such. Luckily, I like clothes."

If I'd heard any bitterness, I didn't now. Just the wife of a busy executive.

"Sounds like Jackie and JFK," I said.

"Jackie? Oh, the Kennedy woman, or Onassis. I never met her. Some similarity, I suppose. Frank is like a president."

Before I could comment on that, the outside door opened. The giant, Tom Nugent, came into the living room with another man. Nugent blinked at me; the other man didn't even glance my way. He walked toward Mrs. Weaver.

"Leonore? Weren't you going out? The Schulers?"

Tall, he was dwarfed by Nugent, but there was no doubt who was in command. His gray suit had a proper vest, his voice was firm and even. But his brown hair was at least an inch too long to be proper, and the suit had a red-and-white polka dot lining. Marks of individuality and a certain independence.

"Your visitor came," Leonore Weaver said. "I couldn't very well leave him alone, Frank."

Franklin Weaver nodded, that would have been bad manners. His left eyelid drooped, some damaged muscle in it, and now the lid twitched. He smiled to his wife.

"Of course," he said, "but you should go now."

She kissed him. "I won't be late."

When she had gone, Nugent stood with his back against the door. I listened to the elevator fade away. Weaver faced me.

"Now who the devil are you?"

I saw that he *was* younger than he looked. The athletic body of a young man under the suit, but his lean face looked older, furrowed and etched in sharp lines. The hard work, and harder decisions, of being executive vice president—and of getting to be executive vice president. Older than his years, power and confidence in the large nose and drooping eyelid. The kind of man who had never doubted he would be the boss.

"Dan Fortune," I said. "I tried to see you at the club."

"Fortune?" His voice was puzzled, tired.

"About the lot lease. Jake Carter has to renew—"

"Incredible!" He stared at me. "All week, twice at my gymnasium, and now even *here!* Can't anyone stop you people from badgering me?"

"I'd badger Berger, except he's sick, or busy, or at home, or on vacation. Take your pick. Mr. Weaver, to you it's nothing. I don't know what it is to Berger. But to Jake Carter it's his life. All you have to do is scribble a memo, and—"

I missed the signal, but Nugent had my arm. That terrifies me. I've only got one arm left. There was no way I was going to resist Nugent. The door closed behind me. I shook all the way down. The doorman met me at the elevator.

"You Fortune? Mr. Weaver called down, you should wait."

I waited, maybe Weaver had changed his mind. He hadn't. The patrol car stopped outside, two patrolmen came in and escorted me out. I didn't ask for an explanation. I'd get one soon enough. Not that I needed one. A lesson.

At the station they let me cool in the tank for three hours. Then I was presented to a captain I didn't know.

"A citizen of my precinct complains that you entered his apartment under false pretenses using your license. You interfered in his business, invaded his privacy, duped his wife. Are you on a case?"

"Not exactly," I said.

He shook his head at me. "I should lift your license, but Gazzo downtown says you're okay. I'm going to buy it, but if you work in my precinct again, try to do a better job."

I got my personal effects, and took a cab. The parking lot was on my way home. I'd tried, but it looked like Leslie and Carter were going to have to wait for Walter Berger.

IMR Center blazed with light as the night people cleaned. The lot was almost empty, but the office showed light. I paid off the cab. A late customer came out of the office, walked to his retrieved car. The bearded man, Carl Pike.

"I met your wife," I said.

"Carol?" He was sober, a little gray under the beard. "I mustn't keep her waiting, then." He got into his car, leaned back out. "The river was nice. I like it." He drove off.

I went into the office. It was empty. The overhead bulb swung idly, three sets of keys hung on the key board.

I went back out. Three cars were still in the lot, one almost exactly in the center like an abandoned island. Near midnight now, traffic still passed on the avenue. A blue neon sign cast shadowy light along the fence behind the shack. Something was in the opening the old man had limped through.

Jake Carter lay on his back, his head in a pool of dark blood, his face unmoving in the blue light.

4

I bent down. He was breathing. Slow and irregular. I ran to the office, called police rescue, and went back to him.

His plain face, swarthy this morning, was like chalk. A livid bruise covered his left cheekbone. In the blue light, blood spread around the back of his head—and around a heavy old transmission that lay against the fence. The blood was dark, a dry crust on it, and . . .

The shadows moved.

On the other side of the fallen man, in the brownstone yard through the opening in the fence. A noise, like metal striking metal. Some dogs began to whine, rattle a pen.

I wished that, for once, I had my old gun. I didn't, and waited, watching the dark night in the dim yards, listening to the traffic still heavy not twenty yards away on the avenue.

There was a step inside the opening, then two or three close together, irregular, like a limp. A squeal of hinges.

I ran through the opening and across the dark yard to the sound. A gate in the fence between two yards was open. I ran through. Loose boards clattered somewhere. The dogs barked behind me. I ran into a brick wall . . .

After a moment I felt my arm, then my face. There was some blood, but nothing seemed broken. I got up and listened.

With the glow of the city all around, the back yards were like a pit of silence. Nothing moved, yet all around something hovered, breathed unseen. The heavy silence itself, the weight of the dark, as remote from the avenues and the sound of traffic as the heart of some vast swamp. A cave of night padded by unknown claws, where men sank and vanished while millions walked the day unaware. The city night itself.

I walked around the yard until I found the half-hidden steps down into a narrow passage. It led out into the side street. Here there was light, but feeble and deserted, and down on the avenues the traffic passed as if at the ends of a tunnel. Footsteps echoed somewhere. Limped? They faded, directionless. If it had been old Ben, he was gone. I went back through the passage and the yards to the parking lot. Sirens were coming in the distance.

A man bent over Jake Carter.

He heard me, jumped back, his eyes scared.

"I . . . came to park. I . . . is he . . . God!"

His soft, fleshy hands twitched as he turned his face away from Jake Carter. A short man, heavy if not fat, he had thin gray hair under a gray hat, a plump pink face anywhere from fifty to sixty. A nervous face now More than nervous, as if feeling Jake Carter's pain.

"Alive," I said, "barely. You know Jake?"

"No!" On edge. "I mean, a little. I park here."

"You came to get your car? When did you leave it? Did you see Jake earlier? What time? Did you see anyone else?"

He shook his head. "No, I came to park now. No one was in the office, so I came out to . . . You see, I have some rush work tonight. I mean . . . What happened to Carter?"

"Attacked, fell against that old transmission."

He shuddered. "So much violence. Horrible."

"Every day," I said. "You work around here, Mr.—?"

"Yes, I—" He blinked, stared past me.

I looked. Someone stood in the blue neon shadows along the fence. Quick, and moved away toward the avenue as I looked. I began to run again, but the shape vanished around the end of the fence. A woman. In a pale green slack suit. I couldn't see her face, or tell her hair color in the blue neon light, but there was something familiar—someone I'd seen before. When I reached the avenue, she was nowhere, people already gathering as the sirens converged on the avenue.

I went back to the short, pink-faced man. He was gone. A man who didn't want to be involved, or did he have a better reason for not waiting? He worked nearby—at IMR, maybe?

Jake Carter still breathed slow and labored, and the rescue truck was close, slowing to turn. I searched Jake's pockets quickly. His wallet, keys and loose money were there. I found nothing else, began to search the area of blue light. A large wrench lay near him. Clean and oiled, it had the label of Carter Parking. I remembered a rack of wrenches in the shack. This would be the largest—a foot and a half long, with a heavy-jawed head. It could be what made the bruise on Carter's cheekbone.

The ground was littered with match covers, candy wrappers, cigarettes and crumpled packages, chewed gum, cigars, Kleenex, the endless debris of an open city lot. I saw the small, oval stone in the sweep of light from the rescue truck's headlights as it turned in, two patrol cars with it, an ambulance behind. A dark amber ring stone with four tiny diamonds in a line in the center. The diamonds looked real. I pocketed the stone.

I stood back out of the way while the rescue team did its work, and the patrolmen kept back the curious who emerged from nowhere, even after midnight, at the smell of blood. As they worked, I studied Jake Carter's unconscious form. He still hadn't shaved, and wore the same garage uniform he had this morning. Whatever he'd been doing all day, he hadn't been home.

A small, neat man in a brown suit stood beside me.

"What happened here, Fortune?"

Detective-Sergeant Lee Parelli. I told him—from the start.

"International Metals and Refining?" he said slowly, looked toward the tower of steel and glass still ablaze with light, dominating the dark lot and us. "You think they had something to do with this? A nothing parking lot deal?"

"They're big and rich," I agreed, "but not everyone who works for them is big, rich, or maybe even making ends meet. Anyone can want more money. Maybe not Weaver, but Berger or someone lower?"

"You never saw this Berger? You or Jake Carter?"

"No," I said—or had I? The pink-faced man looked just right for a nervous minor executive. The fussy type who might handle everything himself and come to work at midnight if he'd gotten behind. He'd said he worked near the lot. I told Parelli about him, about the woman in the slack suit, about the limping shadow and Carl Pike. "Maddox was pretty upset this morning, seemed to take the word 'bastard' literally. An insult to his mother."

"Old Ben. I know him," Parelli said, and wrote it all down in a small notebook. Meticulous, one of the new breed. Not twenty-five yet and a sergeant. I'd heard he'd already passed his exam for lieutenant, was just waiting for an opening.

"The woman could be anyone, but we'll look for that older guy," Parelli decided. "What about this Carl Pike? You said he was drunk earlier. Maybe a drunken brawl, Jake got him mad?"

"He wasn't drunk just now, didn't act suspicious. Anyway, I'd say Jake was knocked down hours ago, the blood crusted."

"Maybe Pike hung around waiting for something, or maybe he came back looking for something. We'll find him, too."

The rescue team and ambulance men had Jake on a gurney, rolling him to the ambulance from Roosevelt Hospital.

"I better tell his wife," I said.

"I'll drive you," Parelli said.

He drove south, traffic thinning at last, but people out on all the sidewalks trying to find some pockets of air.

"Carter's wife," Parelli said. "A belly dancer, wasn't she? A nice piece of work. Leslie Ajemian, yeh. Those club girls mix with a lot of guys—not always nice guys."

"That was years ago. She wanted better, a future."

"I remember her. A smart girl, classy-looking, fit in almost any-where," Parelli said. "Maybe she found something better than the parking business."

When a woman looks like Leslie, has come out of a slum and learned what being a female can get her, it's always possible. Especially if her husband isn't making it. Jake Carter had been awful anxious to renew, maybe worried about losing more than his profit.

Parelli parked at a hydrant in front of Leslie's address on West Tenth Street. It was a renovated brownstone with a tree, polished brass, and a clean vestibule. Carter was 2B, parlor floor rear, the best. Our ring was answered, and we walked up. Leslie stood in the door. It was late for visitors. She was fully dressed in a rich white blouse and tight green slacks that showed off her body, carried a handbag.

"Just got home, Mrs. Carter?" Parelli asked.

"Yes. What do you want, Serg—?" She saw me. "Dan?"

"It's Jake, Leslie," I said. "He—"

Her dark eyes flickered, that was all. "Dead?"

"You expected it, Mrs. Carter?" Parelli said.

"You're not selling tickets," she said, almost cold, and looked at me. "Who, Dan?"

"Why don't you tell us?" Parelli said. "No surprise?"

"We've had some trouble," Leslie said. "We—"

I said, "Stop it, Parelli. He's not dead, Leslie. He's hurt, and bad, but he's alive. In Roosevelt Hospital."

She pushed past us and almost ran down the stairs. We went after her, got her into Parelli's car, drove north. She was silent, only a faint whitening at the corners of her mouth. Parelli was silent for a time, too, glaring ahead, angry that I had spoiled his cheap trick to try to trap Leslie into talking. But he said nothing. The new breed of cop, more on his mind than one case, and he didn't know how downtown would like his trick. Ambitious, and liked simple solutions.

"Where were you tonight, Mrs. Carter?" he said.

"Went to the theater, a bar later, took a walk. Hot, right? No one saw me, I'd seen the play before, no alibi. Okay?"

"Did you talk to Jake today? After this morning?" I asked.

She shook her head. "I called the lot, he wasn't there."

"Is there a jacket to those green pants?" Parelli said.

"No," Leslie said.

Parelli nodded, nothing else, but I knew what he had on his mind. I had it, too—a jacket can be thrown away.

At Roosevelt, Jake was still unconscious. They were readying surgery. Leslie went in. Parelli questioned the doctor.

"Severe depressed skull fracture, Sergeant. We'll relieve the pressure, then it's touch and go. His left cheekbone is broken, not serious. I'd say he was struck on the cheekbone, hit his head on a hard object with a narrow edge."

"Struck with a wrench?" Parelli said.

"That would fit."

"When?" I asked.

"Three to five hours ago, say between nine and eleven tonight. I have to scrub up. Cross your fingers."

In the corridor, I smoked and Parelli scowled. He didn't like it—anyone could hit a man with his own wrench in a dark parking lot. Jake's money should have been gone, simple mugging.

Leslie came out, sat down on a bench. Her dark eyes were distant, in shock, and yet I sensed that she was aware of me and Parelli, tense. She lit a cigarette, her hands were steady. Parelli stood over her.

"Who might have done it, Mrs. Carter, and why?"

"I don't know," she said. Flat, neither low nor loud.

"Who were his enemies? What trouble was he in?"

"No enemies," she said, "no trouble."

"You can't help? No ideas, no suspicions?"

"No."

"What about IMR? He had trouble with them."

"I told Fortune all I know. Who would hit him at IMR?"

Her exotic face was blank. She could be protecting herself, but she was protecting someone else too—Jake. I understood. Jake couldn't tell her what had happened, and in the slums you learn to step softly when someone you love is attacked and you don't know why. You don't know when what you say might make trouble for *him*. Parelli took it another way.

"Don't go anywhere, Mrs. Carter. Nowhere at all."

He walked off down the corridor. I waited until the elevator doors closed behind him, then sat down beside Leslie.

"Jake'll be okay," I said.

"Who knows?" She rubbed at her eyes. "Sure he will be."

"Leslie, I'm not a cop. Tell me what you know. Everything."

"The Chelsea pirate," she said, almost smiled. Then she shook her head. "In the end, Dan, you're a cop, too. Right?"

"If Jake did anything, yes, all right. I won't ask if he did, but someone hit him. Is there more than you've told me?"

"I don't know," she said. "I don't think so."

"Then what happened? A mugging? A mugger can get scared and leave the money, but at the lot alone Jake would've been alert. Someone from IMR seems pretty far out. How could Jake hurt IMR? Why would he worry them?"

"He wouldn't," she said. "No way."

"A competitor? Another woman?"

"You think he needed another woman?"

"You never know," I said. I watched her. "Do you have another man around, Leslie? Who could want Jake out of the way?"

She put out her cigarette. "No man."

"Leslie, I know what happens inside a slum man when he can't support his woman. From the past, when women could get work and the men couldn't. You lived high once. I think it would have been even more important to him to support you. How far would he go to get that lease renewed?"

"I don't know," she said. "He wouldn't do anything."

"You want me to go on with it, Leslie?"

"I don't know," she said again. "Wait with me, Dan."

We waited. A long wait. We dozed in the silent white corridor. Once I went out for some beer and hot dogs. It was past dawn when a tired doctor came out and told us that the operation was a success, he was optimistic. Leslie got up.

"Let's go, Dan."

Not cold, just a girl who'd grown up in the slums of Newark and faced facts, who knew that you conserve your strength for real need. She couldn't help Jake now by crying in the corridor. I hoped that was why she wanted to leave.

We rode a taxi downtown in the hot morning, stopped at her apartment on Tenth Street. A black Mercedes sedan was parked at the curb, a chauffeur in it, and Tom Nugent and Emily Hahn beside it.

Franklin Weaver stood in Leslie's vestibule doorway.

5

Weaver stepped toward us. Not stiff, but awkward, as if not sure of his welcome. He nodded to me, looked at Leslie.

"Mrs. Carter? May I introduce myself and offer my sympathy? Franklin Weaver, executive vice president of International Metals and Refining. I know that you must feel angry at us just now, can only hope that your husband is—"

"He's alive, Mr. Weaver," Leslie said.

Weaver smiled. A young smile, open. "That's good news! Our amends won't be so too little and too late. Is he—?"

"Critical," I said. "You're here early, Weaver."

"I get up at five," he said. "I'll apologize to you too, Fortune, for calling the police, although I'm not so sure I owe it to you. You were out of line. But we'll forget that now. I came to try to make amends for our arrogant behavior. It was unintentional, believe me, but inexcusable all the same. Now we want to renew Mr. Carter's lease at once, today."

"Thanks," Leslie said coldly. "Why the quick change?"

"No change, Mrs. Carter," Weaver said. "For a time we thought we might build on the lot this year, but we won't. Berger should have explained that to your husband weeks ago." He moved his athletic shoulders apologetically. "What can I say? IMR makes such large demands on our efforts, we become so busy. I suppose it takes a shock, sometimes, to give us perspective. We were insensitive and wrong. What more can I say?"

"Nothing, I guess," Leslie said, her voice quieter.

"Then you'll accept the lease?" Weaver smiled. "I'm glad."

Leslie half smiled in return. I watched Weaver, asked:

"How did you hear about Jake?"

"Berger told me this morning. As soon as I heard, I—"

"Berger? Short man, heavy, pink-faced, fiftyish?"

Weaver nodded. "He told me he ran into you in the lot last night. You see, after I'd called the police on you I felt bad, so I got in touch with Berger. I told him to renew the lease at once. He came in, went to the lot to park, found Carter."

"How'd you contact Berger? He came in from where?"

"Short Hills, his home. He actually hadn't felt well, had vacation time coming, so took some time off. He'd felt better soon, so attended to some personal business."

"What personal business?" I said.

"I didn't ask him. We don't—" He frowned. "You think there could be something involving the lot? He did act a bit odd when I called him last night. If I thought—!"

"Does he need money?" I said. "Live high?"

"There was some talk once," Weaver said slowly. "About his wife, not him. Large companies tend to breed rumors. Still—" The grooves from his nose to his jaw deepened, and his drooping eyelid made him seem almost one-eyed, a pirate king. "I think I better talk to Berger."

"Isn't that a little late, too?" Leslie said.

His nose seemed to flash like a sword as he turned. "I doubt if Walter Berger has done anything. I've known him too long, too well. He was my first boss on the executive level, he's a cautious man. But I'll find out."

"We don't need your help or your lease!" Leslie snapped.

Weaver studied her as if he could see inside. "Don't be stupid or sentimental, Mrs. Carter. You're listed as co-owner of your business. I checked that. You can sign. When your husband recovers, he'll need his business. If he's sick a long time, you can sub-lease or sell. Your business needs our lot."

"Yes," Leslie said, nodded, looked down. "You're right."

"I've instructed Miss Hahn there to take care of it. She or my assistant, Mr. Nugent. Anytime you're ready."

He had come to apologize, make amends, and ended by taking charge of the whole morning. The power in him, decisive. Number two or three man in a giant corporation at thirty-seven, probably a genius—ability, power and judgment. Walter Berger was at least fifteen years older, had been Weaver's boss and was now far below him. A man could resent that.

"Maybe tomorrow," Leslie said.

"Anytime," Weaver emphasized.

He nodded to me and walked to his car. Nugent held the door as he got in. Emily Hahn followed. I caught her glance as she bent to get in. She smiled, but it was a thin smile. She seemed to be watching Leslie. The Mercedes drove off. Leslie stared after it until it turned the corner.

"You better get some sleep," I said. "What do you think of Franklin Weaver?"

"I don't know," she said, weary, blinking in the growing sunlight of the hot street. "Maybe honest, maybe all public relations. Powerful, not a man who mugs parking lot owners."

"What about Berger? A shakedown on Jake, and he resisted? Maybe a deal with a competitor, a payoff?"

She thought. "Find out, Dan. I can pay you now."

"Good," I said.

I walked home to my five railroad rooms—hot rooms—and fell into bed with only my pants and shirt off. At least, she'd told me to go on, find out. Then, what else could she have said?

I woke up bathed in sweat, the sun in my eyes, and the heat lying on me like something thick and sticky. I lit a cigarette, and thought about Jake Carter—and about Walter Berger, Franklin Weaver, the bearded Carl Pike, Leslie, all the women at IMR who probably parked in Jake's lot, and old Ben Maddox. Then I thought about food. I was hungry.

I showered and went out. Halfway to the next floor, I stopped short. Something was wrong.

Day after day we do our routine actions without really being aware of doing them. Our minds busy, we go down to the street, never really aware of opening and closing our door. Until something is different. The signal reached my brain—slow, but it got there. My door had opened a shade hard, had closed a shade tight, as if expanded by the heat, tighter to the frame. I went back up. It wasn't the heat.

A tiny electronic sensor was fitted high up between the door and the frame so that when the door opened a signal was sent. Someone wanted to know when my door opened. I went down.

The signal had been tripped, the warning sent, and I didn't expect to see anything on the street. I didn't. I walked in the ovenlike heat to my office. I had an idea why the signal had been on my door. My office was properly locked. I went in.

It had been torn apart, gone over inch by inch by someone who knew what he wanted and how to look. Nothing had been overlooked, not even the ledge outside my one window. From the sensor to the search, a professional. Who wanted to know what I knew. But about what?

I called the building handyman, Eddie Ortiz. For ten bucks he'd put the place back together. I could trust Eddie; he'd done it before. Then I went back down to the hot street.

A gust of cooler air greeted me. Still hot, but clouds were piling up over Jersey, and rain and wind were coming.

At IMR Center the receptionist on the executive floor was startled when Emily Hahn told me to come right in, and closed her door behind us. She seemed to be growing younger each time I saw her, even smaller, the order of her days being shaken by strangers. Her yellow dress was less neat, tight across her large breasts, and her black hair was looser.

"I'm so sorry about Mr. Carter," she said. "You don't think not getting the lease caused it, do you? If we'd renewed—?"

"I don't know, Emily," I said.

"His wife is beautiful, like an actress. Different."

"Armenian," I said. "A dancer. Is Berger in his office?"

"No. Mr. Weaver's out looking for him. He's angry."

"You want to help me?"

"With what?" The automatic caution, protective.

"I want to search Berger's office. Get his secretary here."

"You don't want Mr. Berger to know?" It was hard for her, against IMR, but Weaver was angry at Berger. "All right."

I waited at the elevators until Berger's secretary came up. Then I went down and slipped into his office. It looked like it *had* been empty for over a week, all surfaces clear, the in and out boxes bare, a thin film of dust on the desk. Still, *why* couldn't some assistant handle a small lease? I got what could be the answer—everything was locked. Walter Berger was a man who kept tight control of his work. A nervous type, unable to delegate, or was there some other reason?

I picked the lock on a file labeled Real Estate, found the folder for the lot. It held the original lease, a memo dated four months ago to confer with VP Montrose about possible construction on the lot, and a brief note that read: *Renewal, September.* I looked at that note for some time.

Then I searched the rest of the cabinets and the desk. I didn't know what I was looking for, but I found nothing suspicious. Nothing about the lot, or Jake Carter; no familiar names except IMR people; no suspicious-sounding names. His Short Hills address and phone number were listed exactly as all the others: Mr. & Mrs. Walter Berger—! A pedantic man Walter Berger.

I dialed the number. A woman answered. I asked for Berger.

"My husband isn't here. I'm sorry."

"Where is he?"

"I have no idea," she said, testy. "Try his office."

"I'm in his office."

"You are?" She sounded startled, and hung up.

I sat down at Berger's desk to think. Mrs. Berger had been startled to learn that Berger wasn't in his office. The note in the lot file said: *Renewal, September.* A reminder. What had happened to make Berger forget, or to change his actions?

6

The office door opened and closed fast, and Sergeant Parelli stood inside with his gun out. When he saw me, he swore and looked disappointed.

"Hell, what are you doing here, Fortune?"

He holstered the pistol—a big S&W 357 Magnum. Too heavy for a detective, but a gaudy show. That was Parelli. Disappointed that I wasn't a suspicious character, and he could break the case right now.

"Searching Berger's files. Leslie Carter hired me."

"What'd you find?"

"Nothing much." I showed him the file on the lot.

He looked at it, shrugged, and laid it aside.

"I checked into Weaver and Ruth Montrose. They're clean; nowhere near that parking lot." There was a gleam in his eyes. "Power and money, both of them. Came up fast. Weaver's a kind of genius, I guess. His old man was a small-time lawyer out in California, Weaver graduated pre-law from U.C.L.A at nineteen. He switched to business at Harvard, was an IMR vice-president at thirty."

"Everyone can make a mistake," I said.

"Over a parking lot? With futures like theirs? He's thirty-seven, she's forty-three and just as sharp. Damn, Fortune, they both pulled deals for millions that'd curl your hair. You think they'd make a mistake over a lousy parking lot?"

I heard excitement in his voice. The excitement of an alcoholic hurrying home with his bottle. He'd like to make deals that would curl hair, move fast in the millions. Admiration, and envy and hunger.

"No," I agreed, "but I wonder if they cut some corners on their way up?"

"Plenty," Parelli said, "but not this kind. I'd say Weaver had his eyes on IMR from the start. After Harvard he went with an accountant outfit that did the books for a mining equipment company that sold big to IMR. At the time IMR was losing money in South America and Africa. Weaver moved from the accountants to the equipment company, from them to IMR in the foreign department. When the smoke cleared, he'd straightened out the whole foreign operation, jumped over almost everyone to vice president."

"Montrose, too?"

"No, they moved up together. In more ways than one, if you know what I mean." Parelli grinned, all male. "You know what she is—a mining engineer! Seems she developed some gimmick for making cheaper nickel, and Sam Ross, IMR's president, bought her from another company. I figure he got more than nickel. Around IMR they hint she's frigid, maybe queer, but I smell different. She lives in Manhattan, doormen and supers see a lot. I say she was Ross's girl, now she plays with Weaver."

"She's never been married?"

"Nope, not that I can find," Parelli said. "Two years ago Sam Ross got in a brawl with his board, swept the place clean with his own team—himself to chairman as well as president, Weaver to exec vice president, Montrose to senior vice president. Weaver has women, Ruth Montrose likes power—standard. They don't play with gloves on, but nothing illegal I can spot."

The gleam had changed in his eyes. A different hunger. He wanted to find something against Weaver or Ruth Montrose. Something he could know—and use. A hold. I didn't like that, or him, but it meant that if there was anything, he'd dig it out.

"Anyway," he said, swiveled, "they both have alibis."

"What kind?"

"Good ones."

He was enough policeman to know that there were few perfect alibis. If an alibi was perfect, it was usually a lie.

"Weaver was in his apartment all night after you left. It checks. Doorman didn't see him leave, at eight-thirty he talked to his broker until nine, at nine-thirty he talked for an hour to a government lawyer, his wife got home at midnight. No gap more than half an hour between eight-thirty and eleven."

"Ruth Montrose?"

"Out at dinner with two bankers and a Mrs. Pike. They were seen, left the restaurant at eleven-thirty."

"Mrs. Carol Pike? Was her husband there?"

"No man named Pike. Maybe that's why he was drunk."

"What did you learn about him? Did you find him?"

"Nope. He lives in Short Hills, like Walter Berger. The Millburn cops said he wasn't home, and he wasn't at his office. He's only been in town a month. From California; Ventura. A scientist in the IMR labs in Summit, two kids, the Millburn cops thought it was a gag when I called."

"How about that assistant of Weaver's? Nugent."

"Left Weaver at nine, worked out at his athletic club, got home after ten-thirty. They remember him at the club around ten. Maybe he could have done it, but why? He's not dumb. I can't connect him to Carter. He quit football first time he hurt a knee, used contacts to get with IMR public relations. He doesn't gamble, no debts, lives on his salary. Weaver picked him out of PR a year ago, a big break. He works hard, studies nights. He'd have a lot to lose, not much to gain out of Carter. But you find a motive, I'll work on him."

"Walter Berger?"

"No luck yet. I had the Millburn cops check him, too. He wasn't home. He's been out of his office about a week and a half, until last night. He was at home some of the time, we don't know where else he was. We'll know more when we get him." He swore. "Damn, if Carter's money was gone, it'd be easy."

"So they're all alibied, more or less," I said, "but any of them could have hired it done."

"Hired?"

I told him about the electronic signal on my door, the search of my office. His whole manner changed, alert.

"A pro?" He could see the headlines. "That changes it. We better look for that pro."

"Can I look, too?"

He didn't even hear me, seeing a trail all the way to Washington. I went out and up to Weaver's office. He still wasn't there, neither was Emily Hahn. I left my number in case Walter Berger showed up, and went down to Eighth Avenue. The parking lot was busy, Leslie trying to keep it running herself. She seemed to have a swarthy kid in a club jacket helping out.

On Twenty-eighth Street I walked along the row of decrepit brown-stones. Ben Maddox had gone into the third one yesterday. His name was on the mailbox for the second floor, rear. There was no bell, but the vestibule door didn't lock. I went up. The door was locked; no one answered my knocking. I used my keys. The first one fitted the cheap lock, but the door didn't open. Double-locked. I opened the second lock, went inside.

There were two narrow rooms and a kitchen. Hot and airless with the windows shut tight, piled and littered like some junkyard, yet as bare and barren as the waiting room of an abandoned railroad sta-tion. A narrow iron bed with a skinny mattress and a thin blanket that looked like prison issue—unmade, piled at the foot with old clocks, pots and a broken hot plate. Four stiff old wing chairs. Two heavy tables side by side, heaped with junk from old newspapers to a bird-cage, a corner of one table clear. There were dirty plates on it, but no chair, as if old Maddox ate standing up. No comfort, no warmth. A hermit's cave, and a prison cell.

The kitchen had an enamel table, one chair, empty cabinets and an icebox—with ice. A small cake, almost melted away. One small loaf of bread was open and hardened. The dirty dishes out on the table were at least a day old. Where was Maddox?

I searched the rooms for any clue. There was nothing. Not a letter, not a name, not a personal keepsake. The newspapers were a year old, and his address book could have been half a century. Its pages were brown, the ink faded, and I knew that a lot of the addresses no longer existed. As if everyone he had known was dead, and had pulled their world into the grave with them. An old man, alone a long time, clinging to the fringe of an alien world.

Old and poor and mean. Maybe he had an excuse to be mean. The old don't do very well in today's America. But where was he now? Hiding? Because he was the man I'd chased last night?

I locked the door behind me, went down, and around to the parking lot. New York's long lunch "hour" just about over, the bustle had died down, and I saw Leslie talking to a big, florid man in greasy coveralls. She wore old pants and a man's shirt, making her, with her dark satin skin and black hair, somehow more sensual, and she was angry. Even as I approached, she raged something at the big man. He turned, shrugged, and came toward me. He had big hands as greasy as his coveralls.

"Trouble?" I said. "I guess Leslie's upset."

"Hell," he swore, "I was just tryin' to help out. Run the lots for her, fifty-fifty, while Jake's on his back."

He blinked small blue eyes at me, suddenly suspicious, wondering who I was and why he'd even answered me. Because I'd used Leslie's name, acted in the know. An old trick. The lettering on the back of his coveralls read: Owen Pakula's Garage. The name above his breast pocket was: Owen.

"Johnny on the spot," I said. "The competition. Maybe you tried to get the lot earlier, the easy way."

"What the hell does that mean?" he snarled.

"Maybe you heard Jake hadn't gotten his lease renewed, tried to move in. Or maybe you arranged it, a deal with Berger."

"Get lost," he sneered, blinked at me again. "Jake ain't got a renewal on this lot?"

"You didn't know that?"

"No, but I do now, right?" He grinned. "What was that name? Berger? Yeh, Berger. At IMR. Thanks."

Grinning nastily, he walked away past me. If he could, he'd steal the lot while Jake lay in the hospital. I wasn't disgusted, it was the way it was, but I didn't tell him that Weaver wasn't going to lease the lot to anyone but Leslie. He'd find out.

Grinning a little myself, I walked on toward the shack office. Leslie had gone in. The boy I'd seen earlier came out. He strutted past me, tough, and turned south. The emblem on his jacket was a red devil on a white background with a green border and the lettering: Van Damen Devils. Red, white and green—the colors of Italy. Van Damen Street was in Newark.

I didn't think Leslie had seen me. I followed the boy down the street, and on down to the Twenty-third Street PATH station.

7

PATH is the old Hudson-Manhattan R.R. under the river between New York and New Jersey. A new name, new cars, but the same tunnels that look as if you're riding in a big, old iron pipe held together by big, old iron bolts. You are. A pipe under the Hudson, there a long time, and it makes me nervous, but the boy took it, and I had to tail him. At Journal Square, Jersey City, he changed to the Newark train.

We rode out across the wide flats behind the cliffs of the Palisades. A vast marsh drained by the Hackensack and Passaic Rivers, the rivers and the flat beautiful once long before I was born, but a giant refuse heap now. The resting place of everything fifteen-odd million people had thrown away, the scorched earth of every kind of industry that poured out black smoke and yellow liquid. Still cut by the two broad rivers that are still broad but not still rivers. Rivers are water between trees and mud the color of the earth. We crossed the Hackensack, and it is thick and black, a sludge like lava between banks of leafless gray wood and black slime the color of darkness. Newark is on the Passaic. There are more bridges than river.

The boy took a bus from the station—a bus he'd taken many times before, swaggering through hidden short cuts without a glance behind him. His city, confident. I sat in the back behind him as the bus wound through downtown and out into the wards.

Newark is a sick city, an inner city. A depressed, blue-collar city, dirty, with old brick factories and gray frame houses, asphalt-shingled, four stories high, laundry hanging from the open galleries at the rear. Like the worst of Chicago or Detroit, without their money and power, in the heavy shadow of New York. Once Dutch, then English, then

Italian. Still Italian, so much that the Italian Consulate just opened a new office here, but black now, too—55 percent black, with a black mayor and white anger. Unmelted, two indigestible lumps in each other's throats. Riots, militants and vigilantes. Van Damen Street was vigilante, white and Catholic, the home base of Jake Carter, Leslie, and the boy I followed off the bus.

He strutted his way down three streets, turned into a fourth, and his walk changed. The swagger and strut vanished, he seemed to straighten and shrink at the same time, and went into the rear entrance of a yellow-brick tavern. I walked on past, doubled back, and found a window. In what looked like a combination office and clubroom the boy was talking to three men. Young men, but not boys. A large photograph of State Senator Anthony Imperiale hung on the wall. There was nothing clandestine about the men or the room. This was their stronghold, the whole area mobilized, and they had no fear of interference.

A hand touched my shoulder.

"Inside."

There were three of them, big enough, with two arms apiece. I went inside. The men and the boy looked at my captors. One of them spoke low to a squat, olive-skinned young man. The squat man looked toward the boy.

"You know this guy, Tercio?"

So I'd been spotted the moment I got off the bus. They didn't expect interference, but they were alert for attack.

"Hell, no, Mingo," the boy said, and gaped. "Hey, at the parking lot! I remember that arm. He must—"

The boy paled. I must have tailed him from New York. The squat young man nodded, and one of the three who'd caught me took the boy into another room. I heard the yells begin. No one else seemed to notice. Discipline.

"Why'd you tail Tercio?" the squat man, Mingo, said.

"He was with Leslie Carter," I said. "I know Jake Carter's past, I know where Van Damen Street is. Someone hit Carter."

Mingo looked at my sleeve. "You're no cop."

"Private," I said. "Dan Fortune. I'm working for Leslie Carter." I showed him my license.

"What kind of name is Fortune?" Ethnic differences had become an obsession in Newark. Keep to your own.

"It was Fortunowski," I said. "Polish."

Mingo nodded. "We got Polacks. They're okay, good Catholics." He leaned back. "So why'd you tail Tercio?"

"Leslie said Jake hadn't been near his old gang in years, and there was a gang kid from Newark. Someone hit Jake Carter."

I felt all their eyes on me. Grim eyes, tense and violent. A silence in the room like the eye of a storm.

"You think we know who hit him?" Mingo said.

"Maybe," I said.

A restless silence, the storm stirring. Mingo watched me, almost unbelieving.

"You think we could of hit him? You come here, say it?" He blinked, and then laughed aloud. He looked around at the others. "Hey, maybe we need more Polacks. He's got a lot of nerve, or he's awful dumb."

"I don't have much nerve," I said.

"Yeh," Mingo said. "Okay, what you got in your head?"

I told him about the renewal, IMR's runaround, and Walter Berger's vanishing act. "Carter needed that lot, and time was running out. Maybe he whistled up some of his old gang buddies to try to lean on IMR or Berger."

Silence. Not growing, but not waning.

"Maybe it's not IMR at all," I said. "Maybe something out of Jake Carter's past caught up with him."

"Maybe his wife caught up with him," Mingo said.

"Or," I said, "maybe it was all the other way, you and Jake in some scheme against IMR or someone. Fund raising."

The silence heaved in the room. Mingo waved the others away, silenced them. He looked only at me.

"That all the *maybes* you got?"

"For you," I said, "unless you want to tell me more."

"I'm gonna tell you," he said, "you can take it or leave it. We heard about Carter this morning. Him and the Armenian girl was one of us once, so I sent Tercio over to see if maybe we could help out, maybe get 'em back, too. We was worried, too. We got enemies everywhere. Maybe it was the blacks beat on him. So we checked it out, that's all."

"What did you find out?"

"Nothing much. Tercio talked to our contacts in Chelsea, no noise of any rumble, no black trouble. The Armenian girl didn't want no help. Tercio come home. That's it."

"Okay," I said, "thanks."

I started for the door. Three of them moved toward it in front of me. Mingo spoke behind me:

"Next time, check before you come to Van Damen Street. Give him a tag, Angie, 'n let him go."

I took the small metal tag and went out into the heat and piling clouds. The tag had a devil etched into it, and a telephone number. Two of them followed me to the bus stop, a guard and an escort. As we reached the bus stop, a parked car pulled away fast. But not before I saw the black faces in it.

"They scouts us too," one of my escorts said.

When the bus came, it was all white. The blacks didn't start to get on until near downtown. They sat separately. When I thought of how long they had fought for the right to sit with whites, it was depressing. Then, maybe not. What they had really fought for was the right to choose where they would sit, and one day perhaps they would choose to sit with us again.

I got off with the crowd at the PATH station—and sensed them behind me. Two of them pushing through to be close to me. Young and black. They hadn't been on the bus.

Two more waited at the station entrance. In jackets, African print shirts, and colorful Nigerian hats. The station was crowded. A danger, not a help—a lot can happen in a crowd. I turned and walked away left and fast. It was another mistake.

I was in a deserted factory street, dim under brick walls and the supports of the elevated highways. No way to hide, and no openings except the end of the street straight ahead. I began to run straight ahead, came out into an empty railroad yard on the banks of the Passaic.

As black and thick as the Hackensack, the Passaic oozed sluggish here under rows of low, dark bridges, between banks of factories, dead-end streets, highways, sand and gravel yards, railroad sidings—and two blocks south a narrow riverside park. I ran south. Maybe I could reach the park where people passed in the open, and there might even be a wandering policeman. I couldn't.

A high cyclone fence, barbed wire at the top, reached down and out into the river between the railroad yard and the adjoining factory yard. I hadn't looked back since I'd run; they'd be there. Now I looked. They were there. Two of them, running, and then, when they saw me at the fence, walking. Each of them carried skid chains swinging lightly in their hands.

With one hand, there was no way I could climb the high fence fast enough. I started to run left away from the river toward the opening into the abandoned railroad building.

Two of them appeared in the opening. They grinned at me.

I turned back. I'd have to try the fence. The way the two behind me were walking now, sure they had me, there was a bare chance I could climb . . .

Two more were on the other side of the fence. Just standing there. One with an odd-looking club—a thin handle, and a round head: a Zulu knobkerrie. The other had an iron pipe with a lion-tail tassel swinging on it.

They converged slowly, arrogantly, fluid on the balls of their feet. I looked at the river. An abandoned barge stood at the bank, half sunk into the black water. There's a reason why a rat seeks a corner to fight in—the enemy can only get at him from the front, one or two at a time, in each other's way. I ran to the barge, slipped twice in the black slime of the bank, and flopped aboard.

On my knees, I looked behind. They were still walking, the four on my side of the fence. Enjoying it, waiting for the other two to climb the fence. In no hurry now.

Out of sight, I crawled across the tilted deck of the barge. There was no deckhouse, and through an open hatch only slime and black liquid. The river below the low railing. It flowed like some heavy oil, rotted pilings and sunken objects without a shape sticking up above the surface, violent swirls as if some monster was about to rise. What nameless, slime-bred monsters lived under that surface, fed in the black depths? My neck crawled, and every muscle in my body shrank back. The terrible, primal fear of something unseen beneath dark water, waiting to attack dangling, defenseless legs. A fear like a wall, but behind me there was no way out.

I slid off the barge into the black water.

My legs refused to go down! I started to swim. I swim well, a thrusting side stroke with a powerful kick that eats up distance. Not now. I swam in panic, blindly, the terror of slime-bred creatures below watching through bulging eyes, ragged teeth in four gaping mouths. The current swept me, swirled me, dragged at me to pull me down. The panic, unreasoning, water in my mouth, sucking . . . A shout behind. I took a long, slow, deep breath. Another. Three. And, my teeth grinding, began to swim as I could, forcing the rhythm, breaking the hold of the violent currents.

A barge bore down on me. Horn blowing, faces at the bow peering with open mouths. I fought clear, swam hard to escape the gushing propellers of the tug behind. The barge and tug swept on, their backwash tossing me in the thick, black water. On the tug they gaped down at me. No one thought of pulling me out. Too startled to see a man swimming in the Passaic.

On the far shore, men working on mounds of sand and gravel stopped work to stare.

I was tiring fast, drained by the panic of the black, oozing water, the stink, the tension rigid in every muscle as I waited each second for bulging eyes in some monstrous shape to break that bottomless surface.

The violent currents sucked and surged, swirled by eddies, twisted by rotted objects down under the dark surface. They dragged me downstream, tried to suck me under into the depths where light never reached. I fought, struggled with my solitary arm against the sullen river, and my feet struck an object, or something, under the water. Something solid, yet soft!

I recoiled in panic, in horror, any pursuers forgotten, and swam wildly with all the strength I had left. My feet struck something else, and again, and . . . my hand sank into slime, into black muck. I looked up and I was at the far shore.

I crawled, wrist and knee and ankles deep in muck. I crawled up through that slime, and out on the black shore. I didn't care about the slime all over me, the stink. I was on land, the monsters of the black river beaten. I loved that slime.

8

After a few minutes, I stood up and looked back. I saw one of them in the river too. I looked for the others. They still stood on the far shore. Beyond them, in the distance, a tall man stood with a blonde woman in a short tan dress. He wore dark glasses and a bright African robe like some Zulu *induna*. The woman spoke to him. He shook his head, shrugged. I tried to see the woman's face, but it was too far.

The one in the river was swimming closer, a bold kid. I found a heavy two-by-four. The youth in the river stopped and looked back. He saw that he was alone. One-to-one, I had the edge. He trod water, watched me. Then he grinned, waved, and started to swim back. A salute to a worthy antagonist. The way his long-ago cousins had saluted the British soldiers at Rorke's Drift who, outnumbered 4000 to 100, had held out a day and a night and won in the end.

That salute, and the white woman with the black leader, gave me a flash. Not a racial attack—hired. To put me in the hospital, at least. A pattern was emerging. Someone wanted to know if I knew something, and if I did or not, wanted me discouraged, out of action.

I walked through the grimy streets of Harrison until I was sure I was clear. Then I bought new clothes—the works. At the YMCA I had a long, hot shower, dressed, and called Emily Hahn. There was no word on Berger. I asked for Carl Pike.

"He works in our Summit labs, Dan."

"Who is he?" I asked, "and give me his address." "A scientist. Mr. Weaver thinks he's brilliant, but says he's eccentric, too emotional." She gave me the address.

I thanked her and went back across the Passaic to the Erie-Lackawanna Station. I took a bridge this time.

Short Hills is in the same county as Newark, but not in the same world. A blanket of green from the train. Flowers, and winding roads, and stately houses under tunnels of tall trees. The elegant red-brick railroad station was surrounded by lawns.

The stationmaster directed me to Walter Berger's house. Only a walk from the station, under trees, among thick shrubs and quiet houses. Berger's house was a medium-sized, white Georgian style set back from the road under giant sycamores. One of the smaller houses in the section, it had neat flower beds and a well-tended lawn, but the flowers needed weeding, and the lawn hadn't been mowed in over a week.

There was no answer to my rings. I went around to the rear. The two-car garage was empty. I found a neighbor mowing his lawn. He had seen Mrs. Berger go out in her car a few hours ago, but he hadn't seen Mr. Berger all day. In fact, Mr. Berger had been neglecting his flowers and lawn.

"I know he's busy, but it's poor for the neighborhood."

"Mr. Berger does the gardening?"

"*She* doesn't," the neighbor said. "Sunbathing and lunches with her girl friends, that's Marie Berger."

He told me the address I had for Carl Pike was some miles away. I walked back to the station, called a taxi. It toured through an area of big mansions from the last century, and then stopped in another section of smaller houses in the same Georgian style. I told the driver to wait. There was a station wagon in the driveway.

This house was green and newly landscaped. Professional landscaping. A thick lawn that had to have been sodded, a new coat of paint, and what looked like a new roof. As I rang, I could hear children playing in the back, and Carol Pike answered the door looking harried.

"Hello," I said.

"Hello," she answered. Polite but neutral. Waiting for me to state my business, her blue eyes distracted.

"Is your husband home?"

I waited, and I had the feeling she wasn't exactly there. Her face was as soft and classic as I remembered, but she wore a tighter blouse, and I saw she had breasts. White sandals and short shorts. Not her "chaste" look. She knew she had a body after all. Her face cleared, as if she'd answered a problem.

"I know you, don't I? In that lounge yesterday. With Miss Hahn. You'd met Carl. Mr.—?"

"Dan Fortune. Is Carl—?"

She cocked her head. There were shouts of childish rage from out in the back. She went inside. I followed her into a large living room newly painted a pale blue with white woodwork. She stood listening. The furniture in the room was elegant French Provincial, a good reproduction and all new from the look of it. Not matched, but carefully selected by someone who had style and taste. Outside, the children's rage turned to laughter, and she stopped listening.

"Carl is at work, of course." She looked me up and down, why wasn't I at work? "What do you want, Mr. Fortune?"

"To talk. You're sure he's at work?"

"Of course I'm sure," she said. "Talk about what?"

"He's not in Summit," I said. "The police checked. I'm a private detective. I want to talk about last night."

"A detective? Police?" Not shocked, scared.

I told her about Jake Carter, the parking lot, and seeing Pike there, and watched for a reaction. I got one, but not what I'd expected. She seemed almost relieved. As if whatever she feared, this wasn't it.

"I'm sorry about your friend, fractured skulls are serious," she said. "But doctors are good nowadays. My aunt recovered completely. An automobile accident."

"What was Carl doing in New York yesterday, Mrs. Pike?"

She shook her head. "His work is beyond me. By far."

When she moved her head, the long, auburn hair waved like a thick mane, and I had a flash of that hair on a pillow in dim bedroom light. A key to the contradiction of cool and sensual I'd seen in her yesterday. When she stood still, she was cool, withdrawn, even calculating. When she moved, she sensed her body, aware of herself, sexual. She probably separated love from sex, a social state from a moment of physical pleasure.

"You don't think Carl knew that man? Why, we've been here a month, less. Carl's never been in New York before."

"He was in New York yesterday, he was at the lot with Jake Carter. He was drunk and acting strange."

"Probably too much lunch. He's not used to it yet."

"No, he met Jake Carter hanging around IMR Center, had drinks with Jake. I'd say he was drinking before that, too."

"Would you?"

"You don't sound too surprised," I said.

She touched the polished wood of a love seat, an abstracted gesture. "My husband is a scientist, Mr. Fortune. A brilliant one, it seems. A research scientist, IMR wanted him very much. Something about titanium, I don't pretend to understand. As a man, I do understand him. A research scientist is really like an artist; in daily life he can be quite childish, difficult, eccentric, and impractical. He likes to *feel* new places, he tends to wander around, especially when he has problems in his work. Rather like pacing the floor, except that Carl paces beaches, mountains, even whole cities. He can do that for days, but he comes home eventually."

She smiled. A small smile. "I have to be the practical one, his mother and mistress. He needs me."

"You mean you really don't know where he is now," I said.

She touched a shining chair. "No, not exactly."

"For how long?"

"Since he left for New York yesterday morning," she said, rubbed hard on the chair arm. "I know my husband, Mr. Fortune. He'll come home soon, settle down. I'll calm him."

"You know Walter Berger?"

"Of course. He bought this house for us. IMR did."

"They gave you the house?"

"Oh no, they simply had it ready for us. A small extra."

It explained all the landscaping and new paint. We deal in "extras" today. Bought at cost, or even given by the trades people in hopes of bigger corporate jobs—IMR had a big lab in Summit. A merry-go-round of favors that usually ended up costing the government—meaning middle- and low-income taxpayers.

"The furniture too?" I said.

"Yes, that was Frank Weaver's touch. A shrewd man."

She moved to a velvet-and-wood couch, stroked the polished wood lovingly. Excited by the touch, a thrill.

"How come you had dinner alone at a restaurant?"

"You do snoop, don't you? You mean how come I had dinner with a man last night. I didn't. I had dinner with Ruth Montrose. She had dinner with two men. I enjoy restaurants."

"Where did you live in California?"

"In Ventura," she said, and cocked her head again. "I'm sorry, I must tend to the children."

I heard them yelling violently, a girl and a boy.

"Do you have a green pants suit, Mrs. Pike?"

"What? Why, yes, I have a lot of slack suits. I like the style, not the female uniform of skirts and leg art."

"Tell your husband I'll be back when he comes home."

I went out to my taxi, told him to drive to the Berger house. The children's yelling hadn't stopped. I glanced toward the house. There seemed to be a shadow inside the screen door. Carol Pike still standing there, watching me? I couldn't be certain, and the taxi turned the corner.

Worried? Not as sure as she seemed to be? Sure she had what would always bring Carl Pike back, but not quite certain?

I paid the driver at the corner of Walter Berger's street. The station was only a short walk. I walked toward Berger's neglected-looking house. There was a car in the driveway. It wasn't Berger's car. The screams came to meet me.

Violent screams, not of fear or pain, but of anger. Screams of fury that split the tranquil air of the green, sun-shadowed street. A woman's screams. From the Berger house. I ran toward the house as two people came from behind it. A woman in a sky-blue pants suit that hadn't been bought at Sears, and a big man in a lumpy green jacket. The woman was screaming.

Red-haired and short-legged, she seemed in her late thirties. Small-nosed, wide in the mouth and eyes, she had never been pretty even in her teens. A plain woman, who had never had a good figure, but who was now slim enough for her age, well-made-up and well-tended. She wouldn't dazzle anyone under forty, but for a man with an ego in his late fifties she might be a prize. She was turned out to the nines, blue from shoes to scarf, decked with rings, chains, bracelets and earrings.

As she screamed at him, she tried to grab and hit the big man. He was trying to calm her while fighting her off. I knew him. The big, greasy competitor of Jake Carter I'd last seen at the IMR parking lot thanking me for telling him that Jake hadn't renewed: Owen Pakula. Of Owen Pakula's Garage, and who had said he was going to talk to Walter Berger.

"Pakula!" I yelled as I ran.

He whirled at the sound of his name, terror in his small eyes. He stared at me, his florid face as close to chalk-white as it could get, confused and scared. He didn't recognize me, how did I know his name? But there was more than that—terrified that *anyone* knew his name here. So shocked that he forgot the woman until she caught his coat, ripped it.

With a sweep of his arm, he knocked her sprawling. I made a grab for him. One arm wasn't enough, and I went down in the un-weeded flower beds. Before I scrambled up, he was in his car and had it started. I got hold of the front door handle. He gunned in reverse. The door swung open, slammed me against the front fender, and off into the flowers again.

He drove off, the open door swinging wildly, and disappeared. I got up. The red-haired woman lay where she had fallen, her sky-blue suit covered with dirt, her hair in her face. She lay limp, began to cry, her face suddenly older.

"Dead," she moaned, "he's dead . . . dead—"

"Who?" I said. "Who's dead? Who are you?"

She went on moaning and crying. I went around the house. The back door was locked. I looked into the garage. A door was open on the left side. Through it, I saw a well-equipped workshop. A man lay on the floor of the workshop. On his back, his mouth wide open like the bodies at Belsen. The mind plays tricks, and I heard an endless scream from that gaping mouth, but there was only silence.

He was the short, pink-faced man I'd seen bending over Jake Carter in the parking lot. Walter Berger.

"What's going on? Someone reported a disturbance."

Two Millburn patrolmen stood in the garage. They looked into the workshop. They drew their pistols. One covered me, the other ran out to report.

9

One of them stayed with the body. They didn't let me near it, not until the Lieutenant got there. The other guarded the woman and me. She brushed petulantly at the dirt and leaves on her expensive suit, pushed at the patrolman, her voice peevish.

"I want to go inside. I'm Mrs. Berger, you know. It's my house. He's got dirt all over my suit!"

"Yes, ma'am," the patrolman said, polite to a homeowner, but with a lieutenant to think about. "Sorry, ma'am. The Lieutenant'll be right here."

I expected her to rage, push harder, but she had already forgotten about going inside. She had forgotten the dirt on her suit. She looked toward the garage, and the tears poured down her again as she began to stamp her foot in the blue shoes. Hopeless tears of despair and frustration, that death had come, and that it had come to her.

Two pale blue cruisers stopped on the street, and a gray sedan turned into the driveway. In Short Hills the police came when someone reported loud voices. For a possible murder, a small army arrived led by a stocky man in a cord jacket.

"Lieutenant Kean, Mrs. Berger," he announced. "Chief of Detectives. I'm terribly sorry. A shock. You should be resting. Let me help you into the house."

He took her arm as if it had never occurred to him that if Berger had been murdered, she could be a suspect. She almost smiled, dabbed at her eyes with her thin blue scarf, and hung onto him. She was a chameleon, unhindered by long-range thought, acting to whatever she felt or wanted at the moment. Kean moved his head twice—once at his team, and once toward me. The team fanned out to go to work, and a patrolman prodded me to follow Kean as he led Mrs. Berger to the front door. He bent to her.

"Is there someone you can call, Mrs. Berger? Family?"

He hadn't forgotten she could be a suspect. He wanted someone as a witness when he questioned her, so that, later, no one could say he'd taken advantage of a distraught widow.

"George. He's in Millburn," she said, distracted. "My brother. He doesn't live in Short Hills. He only runs a hardware store."

Kean nodded again, a detective went out, and Kean took us into the living room. It was an expensive room, the same size, and probably about the same cost in furniture, as the Pikes' living room. But as turned-out and color-coordinated as Mrs. Berger—in pastel greens instead of blues. Stiff and blatant, the work of a second-rate decorator who lived on people who could only judge by price. I now knew two places Berger's money went instead of on painting the house.

With a smile, Lieutenant Kean left Mrs. Berger sitting on a love seat, came to me. His gray eyes weren't smiling. The patrolman handed him my credentials. He read them.

"Carrying a gun?"

"Not if I can help it."

"Smart. I have to," he said. "All right, go ahead."

I told him just enough about Jake Carter, IMR and the lot to explain why I was there, what I'd seen of Mrs. Berger and Owen Pakula, and how I'd spotted the body but hadn't gotten near it. I left out the Pikes. Kean scowled.

"International Metals and a parking lot? You're suggesting that Berger was in some illegal scheme? Over a parking lot? He attacked one garage owner in New York, was killed by another?"

"I don't even know he was killed. Maybe he just died."

"Maybe," Kean agreed. "But there was something funny about the way he was handling that lease renewal?"

"He could have just forgotten. He's been away from his office."

"Sick, or busy," Kean said. "Or something on his mind?"

"Personal business," I said.

"Or maybe he saw something in that parking lot," Kean said.

"Or already knew something," I said, and was trapped.

"About what or who?"

He'd worked me into naming names. I tried to think of how to evade, and was saved by the medical report. The doctor, stubby and fast, came in looking at his watch. Kean took him aside. It took some time. Then the doctor hurried out.

He passed a small, erect man who walked into the living room. He went straight to Mrs. Berger, touched her arm.

"Marie?" His voice was steady. "What can I do?"

Kean said, "Mr. Engels?"

"Oh, George," Marie Berger cried, the tears pouring again down her streaked makeup. "He's dead. He's *dead!*"

"Cry, go ahead," the small man said firmly. "Let it come out, sis. Cry it out, then we'll talk about it."

Kean said, "Mrs. Berger? Can I ask some questions?"

"Questions?" She mopped at her face with her pale blue scarf. She stared at the scarf, horrified. It was ruined. Her nose pinched angrily. "George, I don't want anyone here now."

George Engels said, "Can it wait, Lieutenant?"

"I've at least got to know what happened today."

Small as he was, there was something commanding about the brother. Not power like Weaver—simplicity. Uncomplicated and secure. A man who said what he thought, did what he said.

"I think you can do that, Marie," he said.

His voice was quiet, but there was an insistence in it. As if he thought she indulged herself, and didn't approve of that. She was sullen, those mercurial changes again.

"Walter went to see Frank Weaver last night. When he wasn't home by midnight, I went to bed. His car was still gone this morning, so I thought he'd stayed in New York. He often did when he worked late, at a hotel. When someone called me from his office, I did begin to wonder."

Kean looked at me. I nodded. That was my call.

"So I drove to the Racquet Club, Walter sometimes swam on hot mornings. I tried the Summit lab, and called his office again. No one had seen him, so I drove home. When I got out of my car in the garage, I heard noise in the workshop."

Her plain face darkened. The story told me more than she said—that Walter Berger had been a hard-working man, and that she was a woman who dressed in her finery to go out even when worried about a missing husband. Rage filled her voice.

"In the workshop I saw this awful man bending over Walter! Walter was lying there. I knew he was dead! I screamed. The man heard me, tried to shut me up. He tried to get away, but I held onto him. All the way down the driveway he kept saying I was wrong, I'd made a mistake, but I'd *caught* him!"

The anger at Owen Pakula mixed in her with the despair at seeing Berger dead, the realization that he was dead. A conflict, a kaleidoscope of mixed emotions, almost incoherent.

"I hit him! Someone shouted. He knocked me down, the animal. He ran. He knocked that poor crippled man down. He drove away. He . . . he just drove away!" She glared up at all of us, at Lieutenant Kean. "Find him! Arrest him!"

"Try to be calm, Marie," George Engels said.

"Oh, why did I push Walter so much, hound him?" she wailed.

"You shouldn't have married him," George Engels said bluntly. "He was too old, been single too long to handle you. Too much for him, Marie. I could see that. Now you'd better get some rest, I'll handle the necessaries. Is that all, Lieutenant?"

I said, "What did you push him to do, Mrs. Berger?"

"What?" The cloudy, incoherent eyes. "What? Push him? To work too hard, assert himself, of course. Get what was his!"

"You mean he died from overwork? Heart attack? But you acted like you thought Pakula killed him," I said.

She thrashed in her chair, "I don't know, maybe that animal hit him, attacked him."

I looked at Kean. "How did he die, Lieutenant?"

"Poison," Kean said. "Cyanide the Doc thinks."

Marie Berger shrank back. "Poison? But—?"

"You mean murder?" George Engels said, turned on his sister. "Murder? Marie, a man isn't murdered for nothing. What was he doing? Who killed him? What did you get him into?"

"I don't know what you mean, George! I didn't do—"

"A man *isn't* murdered for nothing, Mrs. Berger," Lieutenant Kean agreed. "Can you give us any names? Any reasons?"

"No! I don't know. That horrible man! He did it!"

"Anyone else," Kean said. "Any names at all?"

"I don't know anything about what Walter was doing!" and she burst into tears again.

"I think she's had enough now, Lieutenant," George Engels said firmly. "I'll stay with her; you can talk to her later."

Kean nodded, and Engels helped the crying woman up the stairs. Kean went to check on his team, and I waited. Poison was an odd weapon for a man like Owen Pakula. Still, if there was some around the garage, for moles, woodchucks? If they had known each other, a meeting, a friendly beer? Kean came back.

"Any poison in the garage? Any glasses?" I asked.

"We'll check," Kean said. "You have a car, Fortune?"

"I came out by train."

"I'll drop you at the station on our way."

"I can go?"

"Don't you want to?" He smiled.

"You'll contact New York about Pakula? Call Captain Gazzo."

"Sure," he said.

He wasn't going to tell me anything, and for some reason he didn't seem much interested in Owen Pakula. He dropped me at the Short Hills station, and I got the train for Hoboken. It was dark when I reached Manhattan, hot, the earlier promise of relief gone. I took a taxi downtown to Gazzo's office.

He was there; he always seems to be. An old cop, and an old friend. He'd known my mother, he'd lived his life with all the ways of violence men can think up, and he was near retirement. He didn't want to retire. He said what would he do in daylight? What would he do on a beach, with a tree?

I sat down in the dim office. "Kean called you?"

"He called," Gazzo said behind his desk. "Fill me in."

I filled him in, asked, "Did you pick up Pakula?"

"Parelli's after him. He seems clear, depends on time."

"Clear?" I said. "How?"

"Kean's medical report. Body was stiff all the way, dead anywhere from twelve to twenty-four hours, probably sometime late last night. The wife just never looked in the workshop."

"She doesn't think of much but herself."

Gazzo shrugged. He'd spent his life with homicide, and murderers tend to be self-centered. "No poison in Berger's garage, no evidence of any drinks, so he wasn't killed in Short Hills, Kean figures. Kean thinks he was killed, driven home in his own car, and the killer had to drive away in Berger's car. To some train or bus, Kean reasoned. He was right. They found Berger's car at the Newark PATH station."

"So it had to have been someone Berger visited, probably in Manhattan. Berger's car handy afterward. Any of them."

"Or some Mafia type mixed up in a shakedown, some scheme," Gazzo said. "Got both Berger and Jake Carter. If Carter dies now, we'll probably never solve it."

"It could still be Owen Pakula. Went back to get something."

"We'll find out," he said, closed his eyes. "What about Carter's wife? Leslie Ajemian? I remember her, ambitious."

"She was with me all night, except maybe some twenty minutes between when I saw Berger at the lot, and Parelli and I picked her up. She'd been out, but it's not much time."

"Not much," Gazzo agreed. "Keep in touch, Dan."

I left. Gazzo always dismisses people that way. It's how he gets so much work done without seeming busy. He controls his world, the secret of success. I wish I did.

On the street I thought. Gazzo would handle Owen Pakula and any Mafia types. It was early in the night, but maybe Emily Hahn would be at home. I looked up her number. The address was on the upper East Side, a "safe" area. No answer.

I took the subway up to Chelsea, had my dinner in one of my regular diners—a cold dinner, too hot to eat much—and tried her again. She answered. I asked to come up.

"Well, is it important, Mr. Fortune?"

"I think so, if you're going to be home."

"All right. I'll be here."

I walked along Twenty-eighth Street to Ben Maddox's brownstone. At his door there was still no answer. I used my keys on both locks. Inside, the apartment hadn't changed a hair, except that the block of ice had melted all the way. No one had been near the apartment. I went down and got a taxi.

I rode uptown. Where was old Maddox? Hiding? Because he'd done something last night? Or had he seen something? His rear window had a clear view of the parking lot and the office. Scared and hiding? Or was he already dead, too? Somewhere.

10

Emily Hahn's apartment was on the top floor of a four-story former town house on East Seventy-seventh Street near Third Avenue. Good, but not elegant. About right for a single girl with a good job. She met me in her doorway in a soft, voluminous purple robe that covered her from throat to bare feet.

"Come and get cool," she said, grinned.

I went into a large, air-conditioned living room. A very large room with two window air conditioners. The only room—with a tiny kitchenette and a bathroom—happy and youthful. Giant posters on the walls from all over the world; crazy slogans; animal pictures; bright sling chairs and floppy beanbag chairs; an enormous bed piled with cushions and covered with some kind of dazzling Arabian print spread. A home, all hers.

"How about a drink, Mr. Fortune?" she asked.

"Beer," I said, "and if we're going to drink, make it Dan."

"It'll be hard. You're old enough to be my father."

"Just get the beer."

In bare feet she was an inch taller than I am, but women in soft, voluminous robes always look like little girls to me. Especially if they have bare feet. It makes me think that underneath all that thick, enfolding robe they're naked. The animal desire of the male to enfold the female and carry her to his lair. It's there, and so is the female desire to be enfolded, and it plays hell with the need to be independent people too.

"Here you go," Emily said. "Now, what's going on?"

I took the beer. She had one too. I like girls who drink beer. She sat cross-legged under her robe on a beanbag, like a child in a big blanket, and I suddenly knew she *was* naked under the robe. For me? I tried not to think about it.

"Did you hear about Walter Berger?" I said.

"Mr. Berger? No, I—" She became wary. "What?"

"He's dead." I told her the details.

"Poor Mr. Berger," she said. Her big eyes filled, but she didn't cry. A normal girl, she hadn't known Berger that well, and most of us don't cry over death unless it hurts us. But she was sad, and not just for Berger. "He didn't have a very exciting life, I guess." She brushed her eyes, and then looked up quickly. The rest had just sunk in. "You mean murder?"

"Unless it was suicide. We don't rule that out. Someone could have been afraid to have him found where he died. Tell me what you know about him."

She thought. "Well, he'd been with IMR over twenty-five years, in Personnel and Administration the whole time, never out of the New York office. Once, when Mr. Weaver had just come back from Chile and was going right off to Montana, I heard Mr. Berger tell Miss Montrose that he'd never been anywhere abroad, or anywhere west of Pittsburgh or south of Philadelphia. Sad, isn't it?"

"I think so, not everyone does," I said. "A lot of people never leave their home town even today."

She nodded, almost fierce again. "Come to think of it, I've never been west of Chicago or abroad except once to the Bahamas with four other girls and a tight budget. But I'm going to go places. Even Mr. Berger finally got to California. Maybe Miss Montrose arranged it to be nice." She drank her beer. "He was born in Short Hills, lived there all his life with his dad. His mother died years ago, I think. When his dad died, he got married. I remember we all giggled about it. He was *fifty!*"

"Ancient," I said dryly. "You'd be amazed how young a man of fifty can feel, what he can still do—or thinks he can."

"I'll have to find out," she said, grinned. "Anyway, she was thirty, a Millburn girl he'd known all her life. He certainly seemed happy, livelier, took to snappier clothes."

"That was the only change? Livelier?"

"Well, he did seem to become more . . . ambitious, I guess. He'd been head of his department ten years, seemed content, and Mr. Weaver said he was as high as he'd go. But during the big reorganization two years ago he got angry when he wasn't promoted, so Mr. Weaver made him an assistant vice president but in the same job. Since then he's been, well, restless. Rumors said his wife was pushing him. We heard she didn't like him being under Miss Montrose. One of those women who resent women bosses, I guess. As if all females are the same."

"Tell me about Miss Montrose." I took a drink of my beer. "About her and Weaver. And her and Mr. Ross."

She drank, drained the can. "You're very nosy, aren't you, Dan? Your work, I guess. All right, she and Mr. Weaver had an affair for quite a while, and before that she had Mr. Ross. But don't get it all wrong. She doesn't use sex to get ahead—just the opposite. When Mr. Ross and she split, it looked like she'd lose her job too. Everyone expected it. Mr. Weaver said Sam Ross wanted to fire her to avoid them being around each other, but he couldn't. She was too good, too valuable to IMR. She's our best executive *and* engineer, next to Mr. Weaver, and he's not an engineer. When Sam Ross finally retires, if he ever does, she'll get Mr. Weaver's job when he moves up. And don't think old Sam Ross passed her on to Mr. Weaver. He didn't. She likes dynamic men, and she picked Mr. Weaver."

She unfolded herself from the beanbag chair, went and got two more cans of beer. She seemed to know a lot about Ruth Montrose. Catty? Somehow, I didn't think so. She handed me my beer, refolded herself in the beanbag, drank.

"Anyway, it's over now. Miss Montrose and Mr. Weaver, I mean. At least a year."

"You're sure? He's got someone else?"

"Why don't you ask if *she's* got someone else?"

"All right, has she?"

"I think so; she likes men."

"Would Weaver be jealous?"

She laughed, drank. "That's funny. Frank Weaver doesn't get jealous, Dan. Women aren't that important. IMR is."

"Tell me about Carl Pike. He seems to be wandering around no one knows where. Not working. Is that what Weaver means by eccentric, too emotional? Emotional about what?"

"His work, I think. Not a businessman, or even an engineer. An abstract scientist with the emphasis on abstract. Moody, I think," she explained. "I don't know much about him yet. His wife seems nice, very pretty. I love that kind of classic looks. They came from California somewhere. A research lab, Foley Institute. One of those independent 'think tanks' they have out there. That's how Mr. Berger got to California. He and Miss Montrose went out a few times to negotiate hiring Pike for IMR. He helped develop a process for one-hundred-percent pure titanium, a very important breakthrough. There was some problem about hiring him, but a month ago Miss Montrose got him signed. Mr. Berger was out there, too."

"They went together?"

"No, Miss Montrose went first."

"Not Weaver?"

"No. He goes west a lot, but a month ago he was in Europe. I'm not sure he's happy with Miss Montrose hiring Pike." She laughed. "A damned poet, he says, childish."

"His wife says about the same."

"I kind of like Mr. Pike. The other day—yesterday, I guess—Pike sat in my office for an hour telling me all about the mountains in California. He was nice." She sipped at her beer. "Pike wasn't their first choice. A Dr. McBride at the Foley Institute worked on the titanium process too. He was first."

"What happened to him and IMR?"

I knew the man was in the room before he spoke. A feeling, and a sudden look in Emily Hahn's eyes. I turned.

"McBride chose to work elsewhere," Franklin Weaver said. "I'm sorry, Em, I didn't know you had company."

"Mr. Fortune wanted to talk to me, Frank," she said.

"Dan," I said. "I'd like to talk to you too, Weaver."

For once his mind wasn't on business. He walked to Emily Hahn. Not as if he owned the room, but as if he belonged in it. He obviously had a key, and I knew why Emily Hahn had known so much about Ruth Montrose, why she was naked under the robe, and who for. Not kept, it was clearly *her* apartment, not his. Not boss and secretary, and not powerful man and owned woman. Male and female, friends. She kissed him, and he put his arm around her. Neither of them hiding anything. Weaver looked at me.

"I'm pretty lucky, aren't I, Dan?"

He'd never seemed younger, even his damaged eyelid drooped less. He took off his suit coat, tossed it on the bed. He didn't take off his vest. A man can only be free of himself so far. He patted Emily through her voluminous robe.

"Can I have a beer, too?"

He sat down, relaxed and open. I respected that. I was beginning to have to like him against my better judgment. No, not judgment, prejudice. I'm against big corporations and powerful executives. My fault, not his. I'm a little prejudiced against cheating husbands, too. He read my thoughts.

"You're not shocked, Dan?" His voice was tired, self-critical. "You've got a right to be, after my self-righteous trick with the police on you. I'm afraid no one is always fair or consistent. Then, I suppose you see the worst of us in your work—the cheating husbands, the adulterous wives."

Emily brought his beer. "Frank, don't. Dan came—"

"I won't hide, Em," he said. "I love my wife, Dan, and I need her. We have a complete and full life. I hope no one could tell me from any other Connecticut husband by my family life. I may cheat on her, but I've never cheated her out of anything. With Emily it's a different thing. I need her, we enjoy each other."

"Miss Montrose, too?"

"So? I see you could be a dangerous man. Yes, Ruth and many others over the years. The opportunities happen, I take them. I need them. My wife isn't enough. I'm polygamous."

In a way, he reminded me now of Marie Berger's brother, George Engels. Men who said what they thought, blunt and direct. The way he'd been blunt with Leslie, faced his mistake. Honesty can be disarming. Honest men aren't always the best—Genghis Khan was honest. But he sat there in front of Emily Hahn and said straight out that she was one of many, he took what he could. No tricks, no false promises. That I had to admire. Maybe, under the power and polish, he was more like George Engels than he seemed—uncomplicated, simple.

"I'm not," I said. "Monogamous all the way."

"Many men are. In a way I envy you. I think you must feel an intensity I never do. Only in my work."

I didn't know if it was me or Emily doing it, but he was letting his hair way down. Probably her, part of his need for her, his days spent calculating every motion, every comma. He sounded very human, weary.

"God, I'm tired of fools ruining my work! Rich thickheads who need everything reduced to ABCs, and prima donnas all brains and no sense." He laughed. "You see why I need Emily?"

"Prima donnas?" I said. "Carl Pike, maybe?"

"Him! When I think what—" He shook his head.

"He's important to IMR? Vital?"

"No man is vital; none. He's good, we need his process, but there comes a point . . . Eccentrics! Not with us a month yet, and gone God knows where! Damned annoying." He thought about how annoying Pike was, then turned suddenly to me. "How do you know about Carl Pike?"

"He was with Carter yesterday. I went to Short Hills."

Emily Hahn said, "Walter Berger's dead, Frank. He—"

"Walter?" He got up, put his beer down carefully on a table. He didn't cry, but his drooping eyelid jumped, and the relaxation went out of his lean face. "He was my first boss at IMR. We worked well to-gether, the whiz-kid and the old pro. I passed him, of course; he was a plodder, a routine man. But I learned about IMR from him, the insides, how it functioned. Poor Walter. With an almost new wife. At least, that made him happy. A woman after all that time. I think she was good for him, even if she . . . When did it happen? What was—?"

"He was murdered, Frank," Emily Hahn said. "Poisoned."

"Murdered?" His mind was quick. "Then he must have been mixed up in something? With that Carter man. Probably others."

"We don't know yet," I said. "You saw him last night?"

"We talked on the phone. Twice. You're sure it's murder?"

"Or suicide. When did you talk to him last?"

"About midnight. He called me back after he found Carter and met you. When do they think it . . . happened?"

"Between midnight and noon today, probably early in the morning in New York." I told him the details.

"I'll have to go to the office." He shook his head. "Men aren't mur-dered for nothing. I'll have to audit his whole operation. Tell the police my entire staff is available at any time."

"That's cooperative. They'll appreciate it."

"Cooperative? Not a damn. It's my company. One bad apple . . . you understand. There's no room for mistakes."

"We better find Carl Pike, too," I said. "If we can."

His eyelid twitched. "You mean he could be . . .? But he's only been here a month. It's not possible."

"Berger was in California a month ago," I said.

"Yes," he said, nodded. "So he was."

We both let it hang there. I saw Emily Hahn looking at me. I got the message—I was to leave first. I realized it bothered me. I liked her. But who was I?

"I can only hope," Weaver said, "that if Walter was involved in anything illegal, he wasn't using IMR to do it."

"It makes a difference?" I said.

"If he was using IMR for a criminal scheme, Ruth Montrose will have to answer for it, and so will I, and so will Sam Ross. Some board members would love to have it against us."

"That gives you all a motive to want to cover up anything Berger was doing, doesn't it?"

He didn't evade it. "Yes, I suppose it does."

I left them, caught a taxi home. On my block I checked all around. I saw no danger. Tired, I undressed this time and went to bed. I lay there for a time, thinking that with Berger murdered and Carl Pike missing and Montrose and Weaver involved with both of them, it could be an internal IMR affair. Except for Jake Carter. What was the connection?

A parking lot?

11

The heat broke in early morning, I needed the easy sleep the cool brought, so didn't get up early. About ten, had my coffee, called Leslie, and got no answer. I called the hospital. She was there. Jake was still critical, but every day made it better. I told her about Berger, Pike and Owen Pakula.

"What does it mean, Dan?"

"That maybe Berger and Owen Pakula were into something illegal. Didn't Jake ever talk about Pakula at all?"

"He doesn't like Pakula, but he never talked about him."

"Well, it could be a simple answer. Hang in there. Let me know the moment Jake can tell us anything."

I called Gazzo. They'd found Owen Pakula. He'd been in Scarsdale all night, and could prove it. So much for easy answers. I called Carl Pike's house. No answer. I dressed for comfort, I could be doing a lot of driving.

I had breakfast, rented an inconspicuous Ford from my regular garage, and drove into New Jersey through the Lincoln Tunnel. Route 22 took me to Union, and Route 24 to Short Hills. Even on the grayer morning, the winding green roads seemed a thousand miles away from Newark or even Union. As I reached the Pike house, I saw a racy red Jaguar in the driveway. I drove on, parked at the next corner, and walked back.

There was someone on the side screened porch. The woven fence of the next house was close enough, the approach covered by shrubs. I worked up silently behind it, looked through.

A maid was serving coffee in a silver service. Carol Pike sat in a tennis outfit that showed long, hard legs. Another aspect of her, and I began to think she was a woman who could be, and do, almost anything she wanted. Her visitor was Ruth Montrose. The small vice president looked less plump in slacks and a tweed jacket, the oval face almost drawn in daylight. With her chopped-off hair and dangling cigarette, I could see how Lesbian rumors could start, but she moved with the conscious movements of a female. She watched the maid grimly, and when the maid left, leaned forward.

"So Walter's dead, Frank has his operations under a microscope, and the police are tramping everywhere."

"He seemed such a nice man, withdrawn," Carol Pike said, drank her coffee. "I'd hoped he'd introduce us out here."

"Carol," Ruth Montrose said, "is there anything about Carl we should know?"

"No, of course not!"

"Then where is he? What is he doing?"

"It must be his work, some problem. When he has to think, he sometimes goes off for a time." But her voice was uneasy.

Ruth Montrose heard it. "Without telling you?"

"It's happened," Carol Pike said. "There's nothing to worry about, believe me. I know Carl."

"You're sure? I don't want surprises, Carol."

Carol Pike nodded, the maid came back with a plate of pastries, and I saw the two children. They were behind the house, out of sight from the porch. A boy and a girl, about eight and six, sitting in among a row of trees and bushes at the very back of the Pikes' land. They were being very quiet. Too quiet. They were normal, healthy kids from the shouts and yells I'd heard yesterday. Now they seemed to be sitting on some ledge, or bank, and giggling secretly down at something.

I slipped back to the rear under cover of the bushes in the neighboring yard. There was a small creek down in a gulley. More like a drainage ditch, dry now and thickly overgrown with weeds and bushes.

I dropped down into it, crawled toward where I could hear the children still giggling softly. After a few yards I heard the man's low voice. He was speaking very softly, but in a voice full of drama and flourishes. I parted a bush. Carl Pike.

He sat in the bottom of the ditch, his knees up and his back against the bank opposite the children. They sat across from him, up above, their legs dangling, eating candy bars, more candy and some new stuffed animals and small toys around them. Pike was telling a story about strange little animals called *tee-hees*, and *hee-tees* and *hee-glubs*—part mouse, part kangaroo, part fish, and bat and bee and lightning bug, who lived in the jelly jungle near the peanut butter plain, and one had a wooden leg, and they all drove the lions and tigers and elephants crazy.

A private little story world made up over the years, Pike still making it up as he went along, the children giggling and loving it. Pike seemed sober, smiling, relaxed sitting there in the ditch. But not quite. Not quite sober, and not quite relaxed. Enough drinks to seem relaxed, to tell his little stories with full drama, but not to unclench his left fist, or take the hollow look out of his pale blue eyes. He wasn't dirty or disheveled, but he wore the same bell trousers, low boots, and wrinkled blue blazer he had two days ago, and he needed a shave, stubble ragged around the trimmed beard.

"More, Daddy!" the little boy said when a story ended.

"Shhhh," Pike said softly. "Mommy has a visitor. Is she all right? Mommy?"

"She's fine," the boy said. "Tell another, Dad."

"Will you be home soon?" the girl said.

"A little while. Daddy has some work."

"But tell another story now!" they both cried.

It's hard for children to speak softly, and I saw Pike stiffen as their cries carried through the yard. He stood up in the ditch. On the screened porch, Carol Pike had come to the door out into the back yard. She shaded her eyes, looked toward where the children were hidden in the bushes. She opened the screen door. Pike bent and held his children.

"Daddy has to go now," he said quickly. "It's a game Mommy and I are playing. You be good, think about the *tee-hees*. We'll tell more stories soon."

He patted both of them, turned, and hurried away down the ditch. I crawled for the fence again, stood, and ran for my car. Behind me I heard Carol Pike's voice:

"Carl? Carl! Where are you! You come back! Carl!"

In my car I drove past the house to the next corner. If I was right, the ditch ran under a small bridge halfway up the next block. I was right, and Carl Pike's car was just pulling away. I fell in behind, and he led me back to Route 24 and turned east.

He drove erratically. Too careful at times, too bold at others, and I almost lost him after a near crash when he ran a yellow turning red. It wasn't that he was aware of me, I caught up easily at the next light. A shade drunk, and he led me through Elizabeth, turned north, went through the Palisades, and down into Hoboken.

I followed him right to the edge of the river. An open area of railroad yards, and piers, and low warehouses where I had to fall back. At the edges of the debris-strewn, abandoned rail yards there were blocks of old frame houses. Pike parked behind a big white house that backed on a derelict rail yard. There was no sign on the house despite ten cars parked in back, and no sound except the horns of ships and tugs on the river.

I parked up the street. The houses all seemed empty, no children played. The one Pike had gone into had shades drawn on the top two floors, and the bottom floor windows boarded. There was no bell on the heavy front door. It was ajar, and on the strength of the ten cars out back. I walked in.

It was a small saloon with a bar on the left and ten bare wood tables. An ordinary neighborhood tavern, except it wasn't. The bar was heavily stocked, the lights had Tiffany shades, the right wall was hinged sections that folded back, and through a doorway at the rear wide stairs led up to a distant sound of female voices. A place that didn't start jumping until after everywhere else had closed, and where they offered more than drinks. Despite the ten cars outside, there were only three customers in the saloon—a heavy man in shirt sleeves with an older woman, and Carl Pike sitting at the far end of the bar near the door to the stairs up. The bartender eyed me as I sat down beside Pike.

"Beer," I said.

Carl Pike was lost in thought, turning his whisky glass in his hands. The beer was a dollar. I didn't complain. The bartender walked away, but he didn't forget me. A stranger.

"Hello, Pike," I said, took a drink. It was bad beer.

"Hello." He nodded automatically, pushed his glass for a refill, smiled at the bartender.

His indifference was real. Thinking of his drink, other things, and not placing me at all. Brooding, not even curious that a stranger used his name in an out-of-the-way joint.

"You found the other side of the river," I said.

"Yes." Solemn, as if I'd said some great truth. Then he looked at me, placed me. "Jake Carter's friend, of course. Jake with you?" He glanced around the almost empty room expectantly. "I like old Jake, simple and solid."

He didn't ask what I was doing there. Self-absorption all over him like a river fog.

"Jake's in the hospital," I said. "He may die. Walter Berger's dead."

He drank, nodded again. Reacting not to my words, but only acknowledging that I'd spoken. As if the words themselves didn't reach him through the fog. More than self-absorption, or even booze? He raised his glass in a toast, almost sang:

"To the next man who dies," and drank, put the glass down and stared at it. "Old war movie, bad joke. Sorry."

It wasn't that words didn't reach his mind, but reached it slowly, delayed. His reaction delayed by numb senses, a kind of paralysis. His mind like a small eye focused on some giant object that filled it completely. Tension, some powerful conflict, and I sensed he was near a breaking point.

"Some place," I said to ease off a moment, looked around as three men came in. One thin and black, two white and stocky, all three gaudy. They sat at a table in instant conference. No race here, hustlers all. "How did you happen to find it?"

He shrugged. "Went to school in Newark, the College of Engineering. Twenty-five years, hard to believe. I wondered if it was still here. I guess some needs never change. We used to come over here, very daring. My first girl."

"Your wife and Weaver said you were never in the New York area before."

"Carol? I wonder sometimes if she listens at all." He drank, tasted the whisky. "No one knows everything about someone else, do they? Not even everything about themselves. Not who they are, or what they can do."

"Especially what they can do," I said, prodded.

He didn't react. "Two years in Newark. The poor but bright boy from Scranton, Pennsylvania. Onward and upward. To Cal Tech—scholarship, of course—the brilliant teaching assistant, instructor, research whiz. Perennial student, the little lab in the garage where science could be loved for itself, the pure and exciting problems to solve. Purity and poverty, the independent twins. Love of science does not pay."

"Not unless you can put it in a package," I said. "So Foley and IMR?"

"Foley and, at last—IMR. I'll drink to that."

He did, drained his glass, pushed it out for another refill. I had to finish my beer. Four more people came in. Two short, wide types in T-shirts, apparently together but not talking to each other; a very tall, very skinny black dressed in black like a church deacon; and a blonde woman with a mannish walk in a very short gray dress. A good-looking woman, and I looked. Five-feet-eight, broad shoulders and narrow hips, yet with long legs and curves. Female mannish, the tomboy grown up. The two wide men stood at the bar, the woman and the black deacon took a table, I turned back to Pike. He was staring at me.

"Who are you? How do you know about Foley?"

"I'm a private detective. I came looking for you."

"Detective? Carol hired you?"

"No, I'm—"

"Weaver? Yes, Weaver! Am I that important? Good."

"Jake Carter's wife hired me, Pike. To find out who hit Jake and why. Now I've got a murder, too. You were at—"

Another man entered the saloon. One of the three gaudy hustlers jumped up from their table and hurried out the back way past the stairs and two laughing girls. The newcomer, a big man in a worn suit, followed without hurrying. One of the two broad men in T-shirts at the bar slowly leaned forward and spat a gob of saliva on the shoe of the other one. The room waited, suspended. Someone bumped me. I whirled.

"Sorry, my friend," the tall, black, deacon-type said.

He walked on into what looked like the men's room. I felt for my wallet. It was still there. The man whose shoe had been spat on tossed some money on the bar and walked out. After a few moments, the spitter followed. Those left didn't seem to have noticed anything happening, not even the two hustlers who went on talking as if there'd never been more than two of them. Carl Pike watched it all. I drank my beer, waited.

"You know, they'd kill you at the snap of a finger," he said, wonder in his voice. "Any of them here. Because they think only about *now*. Fear now, greed now, love and hate now. Not like the white-collars, the intellectuals, always aware of the future and consequences. They think in and of the instant. Chilling, you know? Or it ought to be."

"It is," I said. "You were at Jake's lot the night—"

He drank. "You ever kill anyone, Fortune?"

"Yes."

"Yes," he said. "I missed Korea. They say it's hard to kill. For people like us. Not for them here."

"What were you doing at the lot at midnight?"

"What was I doing?"

I went on sipping beer to give him time. He seemed to think.

"One mistake always leads to all the rest, doesn't it?" he said. "One compromise and you go on. Can't stop. Weakness gets to be a habit. The first moment you do something you knew was wrong for you, you can never get it back. You knew it was bad, yet you did it. To please or avoid trouble, afraid to be alone, afraid to lose a small comfort."

"What mistake, Pike?" I said.

"Yes," he said. "Which one was first?"

He waved to the bartender for a drink. I pushed my glass for a refill. It seemed to move away from me. I caught the edge of the bar. The beer glass grew and shrank, hazy.

"You ever hear of Louis the Pious?" Pike said.

"Louis?" I said.

"Early French king, a son of Charlemagne, I think. He was too dependent on women, the books say. It ruined him."

His face grew like a balloon, faded to a distant pinhead. Hell, nothing but a damned sex problem? Trouble with his wife?

"No fault," he said, seemed to be staring at me. "I'm what I am, she's what she is. Neither of us can change. No adjustment, just give in or suffer."

"Pike—!"

It was a croak. From somewhere. I looked around to see who had croaked. Nothing but a fog rolling in. Pike? He was gone, a shape running out the back way, running . . .

The bar fell away from me, crashed to the floor. I saw feet high up, floating lazily, floating away . . . away . . .

12

The rain washed me. Drumming rain, against glass, on wood. I could feel it. Steady, the dripping somewhere, without thunder. A winter rain. Then I'd been asleep all winter. I smiled. A long, warm winter sleep. There was nothing as good, as warm, except maybe . . . I heard Marty laugh somewhere. . . . But if I could feel the rain, why was I warm, and where was Marty?

I opened my eyes. I was in a low-ceilinged room, the rain rattling a single window, drumming on the roof. The moisture bathing my face was sweat. Drenched with sweat, and shivering with cold. I remembered the beer glass moving away, the bar falling. I lay on a narrow iron cot. I remembered my feet in the air, the haze. There was a single bureau in the low room, towels and one chair. Drugged! A low door, closed. I remembered Pike running.

Pike! Then . . . I sat up.

"You just lie down now, okay?"

He sat so silent in a dark corner I hadn't noticed him. A big, fat man in a gray shirt and brown pants, his huge hands hanging curved at his sides. He had a small head and an anxious face as if trying to solve some problem. A perpetual problem he would never solve, or even understand. The face and voice of a nine-year-old in the forty-year-old body of a man.

"Where am I?" I said. "What the hell am I doing here?"

"I don't answers no questions," he said, recited, and then pleaded, "Okay?"

I got up and went to the window. I saw the railroad yard, the river in the distance. I was in a rear room of the same house. I felt dizzy, sick. I held to the window frame, and then the big man had me by the neck. He picked me up by the neck like a chicken, carried me back to the cot, dropped me on it. He handed me a glass of liquid. I tried to knock it away, but he moved too fast. He held my neck again, squeezed as if he'd snap it like a blade of grass. I drank.

All dark, the rain steady. I opened my eyes slowly. I didn't move. Far off I heard the sounds of music and many people. Nearer, in other rooms, there was low laughter, male and female, and soft cries. The after-hour joint was in full swing. I had been here at least twelve hours! I got up, went to the door.

"You got to not go."

He had the ability to sit utterly still, utterly silent. In the dark I'd missed him. He hit me in the face. I went down. He hit me again on the floor. Again. Picked me up and hit me. I felt like a limp rag doll in his grip. There was an odd sound. He was crying. Blubbering each time he hit me. Horror on his blank face, hating to hit, but a fear more than the horror. Fear of the ones Pike had said would kill at the snap of a finger. Pike!

He hit me on the stomach. I lay gasping. He carried me back to the cot.

Twice more it was dark, once light. I was starving. I drank the liquid. The last time he left and I vomited it up. Most of it. Lay weak and thinking how long? A day? A week?

Light and no rain. My head was clearer, most of the drug vomited the last time. This time I made myself lie motionless while my eyes carefully searched every hidden and dim inch of the small room. He wasn't there. I got up and tried the door. It was locked. My suit jacket was on a chair. They hadn't taken my keys. A cheap room lock, I opened it, and stepped out into a narrow upstairs hall.

Closed doors lined the narrow hall. I heard women singing behind the doors, coughing, the morning sounds of washing. I turned toward the stairs. A girl in a yellow robe came out of a room. Not twenty. She saw me, screamed. I tried to plead with her to stop, be quiet, but only a whispering croak came out. My voice! It scared me more than the girl's screams. It shouldn't have. Weaving and staggering, I pushed past the girl and into his grip.

He spun me, got a full nelson, and carried me, feet dangling, back to the small room. He dropped me on the cot.

"Please," he said, hit me on the mouth. "Don't try. I gotta keep you for Doctor Faith. Please."

He hit me again. "Please."

Again . . .

It was dark again, a moon up. My brain felt clearer. The retarded goon had forgotten my drink the last time. Or did someone have some other plan for me, no more need of the drug?

Head clear, I knew I was almost starving. I knew I'd been here a long time. My face hurt. I could wonder what was going to happen to me next. I knew I could never leave here. I could die here. In a way, I wished my head wasn't clear. I concentrated on the pain of my face. There was a mirror.

The battered face looked back at me in the moonlight. No wonder that girl had screamed. I thought of the outside. The window was nailed shut, three stories up, a narrow yard below, and then the derelict rail yard. Two stories down the roof of a small back porch jutted out.

I heard him coming, heavy and flat-footed. I ran back to the cot. What was the name he'd used? What . . . ? Doctor . . . Doctor Faith! He came in, laboriously locked the door, panting. I made my voice weak. It wasn't hard—a whispering croak.

"Tell Doctor Faith it's all right. It's all right."

He turned. "Huh?"

"Doctor Faith is right," I said. "I'm sorry I did it."

"Sure, sure I will," he said, eager. "Sorry?"

"For trying to get away. I was wrong."

"Sure," he grinned, happy. "That's good. Okay."

"But I'm hungry. Doctor Faith says feed me," I said.

"Doctor Faith?" He was confused.

"How about a cigarette? Both of us. In my coat, if they're still there."

"Hey, I don' steal. Cigarette, sure."

He got the package, fumbled with it. I took it gently, smiling. He was used to people taking things, helping him. I lit two, gave him one, smiled at him. He grinned. I said:

"Fine man, Doctor Faith. Do you like him, too?"

"My friend! Yessir. A prophet, got the word. Nobody can fool Doctor Faith. He says I'm smarter than people say."

"Then you better get my food. Doctor Faith told you to."

"He told me?" Alarmed, trying to remember.

"Of course, don't you remember? Doctor Faith said feed me."

He remembered. Time and place meant nothing.

"Yeh, sure, I remember. Food, I go get some."

He hurried out, locking the door. A doglike reflex. I didn't care about that, I wasn't going to try that way again. I tore the bedding off the iron cot, dragged the cot to the window with its legs still down, and lifted one end onto the sill. From the other end I smashed it through the window.

Sweating, I held the bed with my lone arm, braced my feet, and eased it out until the legs caught on the sill and it hung straight down. Praying the legs didn't slip, I climbed the springs down to the end, and let myself go into space holding to the head bar. I dropped the remaining story to the roof of the small porch, rolled off to the muddy ground. I was up and over the fence into the derelict railroad yard before I heard the bellow behind me.

I didn't looked back. He would be a fat white face at the top floor window, insane with rage, betrayal and fear of Doctor Faith. I ran—and I knew who Doctor Faith was: a tall black man who looked like a deacon and bumped at bars to slip mickeys into beer. Another hired hand, and it had to be Carl Pike who'd hired him to hold me. Carl Pike, Walter Berger and, somehow, Jake Carter. Jake had to be mixed up with Pike and Berger. He had to know Carl Pike a lot better than he'd told me—or he had to know something much more *about* Carl Pike. He had lied to me

I ran in the moonlight along rails that led to nowhere. Piers in the river, dark and silent; abandoned platforms; yards of junk. A maze of rusted, crumbled refuse, and they wouldn't spot me here. Everything is good for someone, even pollution.

I reached a street I knew, and in the shadows of the buildings made my way to the Erie Lackawanna Terminal and PATH. The terminal clock read two A.M. A newspaper told me it was Saturday night. I'd been in that room since Thursday noon. I went into the terminal and had six hot dogs and three glasses of milk while the people stared at a coatless man with one arm and a battered face.

On the train I huddled in a corner, still hungry, cold, and shivering from more than either. But by the time my stop came at Twenty-third the hot dogs had taken effect and I felt better. I rode on to Penn Station, and there caught a taxi to Roosevelt Hospital. Jake Carter had lied about how he knew Carl Pike, one way or another. He either knew Pike, or knew something about Pike.

I went up to the floor, found Leslie alone in the waiting room. She looked at my face, then looked away.

"Jake lied to me," I said. "He lied about knowing Carl Pike, about who Pike was. Did you lie about Pike, too?"

"No," she said, "I didn't lie."

"Can I talk to Jake yet? Maybe he doesn't want to talk."

"No," she said, "you can't talk to Jake. He's dead."

I sat down. She lit a cigarette.

"He died an hour ago. I didn't feel like going home yet," Leslie said, smoked. "Just slipped away, never regained consciousness." A smile, bitter. "He never knew what hit him, I guess you'd say. One man by himself hasn't got much chance."

I lit a cigarette. She looked out the high windows at the city that never stopped moving.

13

We buried Jake Carter three days later. There had had to be an autopsy. It showed nothing more than the broken cheekbone and the broken skull that had killed him. A Tuesday, sunny again outside the church but a storm brewing down in the Atlantic, the changeable season. My face looked better, and they'd already buried Walter Berger in Short Hills, half of IMR and the community there. They kept me away from Marie Berger, but Lieutenant Kean said he'd look for Carl Pike.

Jake's funeral was smaller. He hadn't been a pillar of a community and a corporation. It was in Newark where his parents still lived. Leslie didn't stand with them; they blamed her. A few gang leaders turned out, Mingo among them, as much out of suspicious observation as respect. Leslie stood with me, and Captain Gazzo, and Jake's sister, who cried. Leslie didn't cry or say much. Gazzo stood uncomfortably. He'd been to a lot of funerals, and hated all of them. He said life deserved more than the tears of people you hardly knew. It deserved silence.

The priest eulogized, and I said, "Anything on Pike?"

"No," Gazzo said. "Kean had that house raided, nothing there when the Hoboken boys arrived, of course. They picked up the dummy, got nothing from the poor guy. Doc Faith's vanished. He's an old hand, he'll come back and deny when it cools down. You've got no proof, he'll be back in business in a month."

"What else on Jake? It's your homicide now."

"Looking for clues, witnesses, and old Ben Maddox. So far Weaver says Berger's department looks clean, so does Parelli. The runaround was just that—Berger forgot about the lease."

"Why?" I said.

"Who knows? People forget."

"Parelli likes big corporations," I said.

"All right, that's enough. Our accounting experts don't like corporations and Berger's books are clean so far, Dan."

Franklin Weaver appeared near the end of the ceremony, with Emily Hahn, Tom Nugent and Ruth Montrose. Jake's parents were impressed when they saw him. So was I. Nugent and Ruth Montrose stood at the back, Emily Hahn came to Leslie and me. Weaver strode straight down the aisle to the open coffin.

He didn't glance right or left, his lean face almost grim. At the coffin he kneeled, bowed his head, and remained like that in silence for some moments. Then he raised his head, firmly, and looked at Jake in the coffin as if saying farewell to a real person, someone who had existed, a part of us all. He stood, turned, and marched straight back up the aisle the way he had come. No falseness, no lip-service to convention, unsentimental. A man with a code and the strength to live up to it, to do what he felt was right, unconcerned with the approval of others. Like some duke born to the manor and style, certain of right and wrong, of who and what he was.

They closed the coffin, and we went to the cemetery, and then it was over. For Jake, and for us. I offered Leslie a ride home in my rented Ford.

"I'll buy you a drink," I said. "For Jake. No charge."

"Thanks, Dan, but I've got a ride. Thanks for everything."

"Not yet," I said, "I haven't finished yet."

She looked around the sunny cemetery. "You don't think it's finished, Dan? Maybe it should be."

"Don't you want to know? Who and why?"

"I'm not sure I do," she said.

"Life has to go on?"

"It goes on, Dan. One way or another."

"What way? You've got a business, a future. Jake's."

"Have I?"

"Sell out?" I said. "Jake worked to build it."

"Jake's dead."

"Sure," I said. "Well, I'll come and see you soon. A few days. Then we'll have that drink."

She smiled. "I'll think about the business, Dan."

She walked away toward the rows of cars. I followed more slowly. I felt uneasy. Jake dead, Leslie was moving on? Yes, all right, a strong woman—but it was as if she knew where she was going already. Somewhere she had known for a long time, using me after all? The lie not from Jake, but from her? She'd been out that night.

"Mr. Fortune?"

Carol Pike leaned out of Ruth Montrose's red Jaguar. In proper black, with a brimmed felt hat, but slim black and looking like a queen. For a moment I wondered about Ruth Montrose's romances. Traveling everywhere with Carol Pike wouldn't help stop the rumors. Then, Montrose was Pike's boss.

"Mrs. Pike," I said. "Any news of your husband?"

"Carol," she said, smiled, then frowned. "No, nothing. I'm really becoming alarmed. I heard you saw him, talked."

"We talked," I said. "About Louis the Pious."

"I see, yes. We have our small problems."

"Most people do. He asked if I'd ever killed anyone, talked about a mistake. One mistake and you can't stop."

"Did he? Was he drunk?"

"Yes, some, but I had the feeling he knew what he was talking about, brooding. You know what he was talking about?"

"No, I really don't. I suppose we never know everything about someone else, not even our husbands."

"That's what he said. He thought you hired me. Or Weaver."

"I see."

"Why is he hiding, Carol?"

"I don't think he is hiding. He's just off thinking."

"He hired a man to keep me prisoner."

"You're so sure Carl did that?"

Was I sure? Not absolutely. I had a vision of him running away in my drugged fog. Or just getting out of that bar?

"I don't have proof," I said.

"Then you'll keep looking? I'm afraid he could get hurt, or be hurt already. In places like that one."

In places like that one? It hit me—how did she know?

"Who told you I'd seen Carl? How do you know?"

"Mr. Weaver told me. Why?"

Ruth Montrose came up then. Her nod to me was curt as she got into the Jag and they drove off. How had Weaver known I'd seen Pike? I'd only told Gazzo, Lieutenant Kean and Leslie. Gazzo and Kean had no reason to tell him, and every reason not to with IMR still involved. I looked for Leslie. She was gone. I went to my car.

I parked in front of Leslie's apartment on West Tenth, rang the bell. She answered, and I went up two steps at a time. Her door was open. She was on her couch, a drink in her hand.

"Leslie," I said, "how did Frank Weaver know I'd seen Carl Pike? Unless he was—"

"Weaver?" she said.

A man's voice said, "Because she told me, Dan. How did you think I knew? I really wasn't there, you know."

But I'd already forgotten that idea. I looked at both of them, and I knew. There in the way Weaver leaned easily against the mantel, a drink in his hand too. In the way Leslie was already out of her black and wearing a sleek red dress that outlined her dancer's body. Heavier than the topless days, but maybe all the better for it. The red dress set off her pale brown breasts, her dark eyes and black hair. I spoke to her.

"When did you tell him?"

"A few days ago," she said. "I owe you some money."

"Come out for that drink," I said. "We'll talk."

"Eight days, isn't it? Fifty a day?"

"Jake's been buried less than an hour!"

"I can give you part of it."

She stood to get her handbag. Weaver just leaned there. She wanted me out, gone. Now.

"A hundred a day," I said. "That's my regular price."

Her eyes flashed. "Is my life your business, Dan?"

"No," I said. "You don't have to pay me."

Weaver said, "I'll pay him. Call it a loan."

"Or a down payment," I said.

"Stop it!" Leslie said.

We stood there in silence. They were only waiting for me to go. I was in their way, the uninvited voice.

"How long after Jake died?" I said. "A day? A few hours?"

Weaver said, "We didn't plan it, Dan. There was the lease, hospital meetings, some drinks. I felt guilty about the lease and Berger, so I visited the hospital. We talked, it happened."

"You're sure you didn't already know each other?" I said.

"You really think Frank's a man who'd kill over a woman? Any woman?" Leslie said, contemptuous. "And I never sneaked around in my life, I never will. He had nothing to do with what happened, and you know it."

"Case closed," I said, "and not much advantage in mourning. Maybe you're right."

"Go away, Dan," Leslie said.

I heard someone come in behind me. Nugent. I had nothing more to say anyway. Weaver told Nugent to write me a check. I took it. Leslie didn't look at me again.

I went down to the street. The big Mercedes was there, waiting for the master and his new woman. Emily Hahn was there, too. Damn Weaver! Emily tried a smile that didn't come off. She didn't want to talk, and neither did I. I went home.

Were they lying? I remembered the way Emily Hahn had looked at Leslie on the street that first day when Weaver came to make amends. Had Emily known something, or had she just known Weaver? I'd find out. About them, and about Carl Pike. At least, I had the money to go to California. If I packed fast, I could still make a one-thirty flight.

14

I called an old contact in Hermosa Beach to have a car waiting, landed in Los Angeles at four P.M. Pacific Time, and was on the road in the fast Buick by four-ten. I took the Ventura Freeway, U.S. 101, through the hot, inland valleys. Route 1, the old Coast Highway, was on the ocean and a lot nicer, but I hadn't come for a swim or dinner in Malibu.

Once over the high pass and through Camarillo and Oxnard it was cooler, but the real cool, and the smell of the sea, didn't come to meet me until Ventura itself. I've driven north from L.A. many times over the years, but I've never lost the sense of vast peace, freedom, that comes to meet me with the sea at Ventura. Ventura itself is a small city—40,000-plus—on the coastal plain of the Santa Clara River, ringed by mountains to the west, north and east, and ruined by freeways.

Foley Institute was off the branch freeway north toward Ojai. A mile up a side road on the slope of a dry, brown mountain. Three sprawling, Spanish-style buildings around a large green lawn and an old adobe fountain. Small houses clung to the slopes in the distance, more dotted the dry chaparral below, were hidden under dusty green oaks and tall eucalyptus. A silent landscape, open and peaceful, with hidden hollows where it was always cool under the trees. A sense of timelessness, slow and natural.

I parked behind the main Foley Institute building in a macadam parking lot, and the sense of peace and nature vanished. Foley Institute was now; busy and crisp. Surrounded by cars, humming with air conditioners, and guarded by men in uniform. Advanced work, government contracts. I asked to see the head man. The guard called his secretary. I gave my name, mentioned the police, and added a touch of IMR. That did it.

"Dr. Foley says go to his office. Here's a badge."

A machine took my picture and made a badge of it in seconds, the guard directed me to the right corridors. I went along in quiet cool between closed doors. No one lingered in the halls. I could hear voices and humming machines, but I met no one until I went through a door marked Director. Three young ladies bent over typewriters, an older lady ushered me into a large, sunny office with a thick carpet, sealed windows and a mammoth desk with a big, shaggy, completely bald man behind it.

"Sit down, Mr. Fortune," he said, brisk. "Drink?"

"I'll take a beer."

"German all right? Loewenbrau?"

I nodded, and he went to a cabinet that opened to reveal a well-stocked bar with refrigerator. Around it were easy chairs, a couch, and two coffee tables like a small living room, and a large board with 8 by 10 glossies of the Foley staff with complete background details. Public Relations. Dr. Foley had the precise manner of a scientist, the shaggy clothes, a deep groove above his nose and a distracted expression as if he was working out some problem. But he was PR all the way.

"Now," he said, after giving me my beer, taking one back to his desk, tenting his hands, "let's talk about IMR and the police. Some mistake, of course. Just what is your position?"

I told him. My position, and the general outline—not the details. Berger's murder; Pike being missing, but not that I'd seen him, talked; Weaver and Ruth Montrose's concern.

"There's a Jake Carter, too. The name mean anything?"

"Nothing at all." He shook his head slowly. "Walter Berger dead? Murdered? And some people say no crime wave!"

"You knew Berger well?"

"No, hardly at all. Not my side of the street, his work. I know Carl Pike very well, of course. Brilliant man, but moody. I must say that, although we were sorry to lose him. We could hardly match IMR's offer, or their facilities."

"Were he and Berger close? Out here?"

"Oh, no. Berger simply came out with Ruth Montrose when she interviewed Pike and McBride."

"But McBride was first choice?"

"I can't say who was first choice, but Miss Montrose did seem to be leaning toward McBride until—" He sighed.

"Until he chose another company? Why?"

Foley pursed his lips. "I'd better give you the data in sequence. About six months ago, McBride—Dr. James McBride, a very top man—and Pike made a break in titanium. One-hundred percent pure! Only a beginning, but very promising. Naturally, IMR got wind, sent Ruth Montrose and Berger out. There were discussions; Montrose is a first-rate engineer. She seemed to concentrate on McBride. Pike was the junior, didn't have the solid background Jim McBride did. A lot of academic time, private research, and only with us part-time. Then—"

The groove in his forehead deepened. "Another company, Titanium Development Incorporated, was interested in McBride's work. A much smaller company, in Santa Barbara up the coast, but with very fine specialized research. Jim McBride went up there, seemed interested, but I'm not sure he ever actually made a decision before the tragedy."

"Tragedy?" I sat alert.

"McBride apparently took a walk on Titanium Development's grounds. They're on a high bluff over the ocean. A known bad spot, I'm told. He fell, died on the rocks below instantly."

"When?" I said, leaned forward. "When did it happen?"

"A little over a month ago. Sad and unbelievable."

"Then IMR hired Carl Pike?"

"Ruth Montrose was out here the next day."

"Walter Berger, too?"

"No, she came alone then."

"You're sure? He was supposed to be in California."

"I'm certain he wasn't here."

"Was there an investigation of McBride's 'accident'?"

"Some routine questioning, not much."

"How did Pike and McBride get along? Any jealousy?"

Foley looked out his windows. "I'll be frank, Mr. Fortune. I'm not fond of Carl Pike. He and Jim McBride got along, but they weren't friends. Too different. McBride was a dedicated scientist, but practical. A hard-working man with purpose and direction. Carl Pike is erratic. A good scientist, but in odd directions, quirky. The kind of man who thinks the world's problems, like pollution and poverty, can be solved by pat, simple answers. Men like that are my pet peeve."

When a man tells me his pet peeve is people who have pat, simple answers to the world's problems, I find that 99 percent of the time he's a man who's doing fine the way things are. The problems don't touch him personally, he doesn't much want change. The poor, weak and beaten will take any answers they can get, unless they've been programmed to reject an answer beforehand. But he seemed to know Carl Pike.

"Did McBride have a family?"

"A wife. She took it hard, I'm afraid. I'm not even sure where she is now, but my girl has her address." He watched me over his hands. "I'm sure your suspicions are wrong, Fortune."

"Thanks for the beer," I said.

I drove into Ventura. James McBride's house was on a quiet street, an older house that looked deserted in the evening sun. The lawn was overgrown, some outdoor chairs at the side had fallen over, and a hammock lay where it had slipped from one support. I rang the front door bell for some time. There was no answer, no sound or movement inside. The door was locked.

In my car I found a telephone booth, called Dr. Foley's secretary. She gave me Carl Pike's old address, and directions how to find it. I needed them. It was a sharp, unmarked exit from 101 about four miles north where the mountains towered close to the highway and the sea. A frontage road curved back under 101 through a deep barranca.

The barranca cut steeply down from the rough, dry mountains, and opened out to the ocean between sloping cliffs. The road dead-ended above the beach, and a colony of small houses were scattered along the slopes. Children played in sandy, cluttered yards, and men fished the beach.

Pike's house was one of the largest, high up and with an attached garage, but still a small house. The yard was rustic and irregular, with an indifferent lawn but nice flower beds, and a mammoth red bougainvillea that climbed all over the house and garage. I parked on the road behind a yellow Impala, and climbed up to the house. There was a brick patio at the side, with a sweeping view of the sea and beach and mountains behind. A beautiful spot, but the house was little more than a cottage.

The door was open, a real estate lock-box on it. Inside, a small living room was sunny and pleasant, the furniture all odd pieces bought, from the look of them, secondhand. A small, closed porch with the same haphazard furniture, no dining room, and a large kitchen with a breakfast area. The garage opened off the kitchen. It was completely filled by a laboratory—a desk, workbenches, glassware, electronic equipment. Why had Carl Pike left it all? Because at IMR he had better? Here he'd needed his lab because he could only get part-time work?

I went back into the cottage, turned down a hallway that led toward the rear. A woman appeared coming from in the back. Tallish, with broad shoulders and narrow hips for a woman, about one hundred forty pounds under a long, loose raincoat that hid any breasts or curves. She wore an ungainly man's felt hat, dark glasses, and an annoyed expression.

"I'm sorry, the house is sold. The listing should have been dropped. Those stupid multiple people."

"I'm not buying," I said. "Is this furniture the new owner's or the Pikes's?"

"The Pikes. I was to send it on, but now they've told me to sell it. All except the laboratory. Are you interested?"

"No. How long did they live here?"

"About three years. You're not a friend of theirs?"

She had a clipped voice like someone used to being sharp and brief. No nonsense, direct and to the point. There was something about her. The way she moved, walked.

"Credit check," I said. "Are real estate agents often responsible for shipping furniture from houses they sell?"

"No, but I know the Pikes. A favor."

"Who told you to sell instead of ship? Carl Pike? In person, maybe? You've seen him recently?"

"No, I haven't. Have you, Mr.—?"

"Fortune," I said, smiled. I liked her style. "So you knew them? They got along? Happy with this house?"

"He's the moody type, but she seemed able to handle him. The house was small for them, but all they could afford. I understand they've done much better in the East."

"Much better," I said.

"I'm glad," she said. "Now I leave, so out you go first."

I went. I drove under the freeway, passed the entrance, and turned into a dirt road. I waited out of sight behind some trees. I'd never gotten her name. I hadn't asked, but real estate agents don't usually wait to be asked. They hand out their cards like confetti.

The yellow Impala appeared, turned onto 101, and headed north. I drove back, went up to the small house, used my keys. I skipped the front rooms, I'd seen them, went to the back. There were three bedrooms and two bathrooms.

Two were children's rooms with the same old furniture and marks all over the walls where posters and other treasures had been taped and tacked. The treasures had not been left. Casual rooms with well-used doors to the patio as if the kids had lived half outdoors. Their closets were empty.

The master bedroom had twin beds. One side had a decent, if inexpensive, matched set of chest-of-drawers, dressing table, night table and chair. The other side had more secondhand furniture. There were two closets, both empty. The bathrooms were empty and silent—except for a slow drip in the stall shower of the master bathroom. I opened the door.

The stall was empty.

I went back to my car, took the freeway south to Ventura and the Pierpont Inn. In the lounge I had a beer, and thought about the Pikes and their beach cottage. It was a big jump to Short Hills in more than distance—about as far as IMR was from a part-time assistant job at Foley Institute. And . . .

"Sorry!" A man bumped me as he passed. "Excuse me."

I froze, and had a vision of the black deacon in the Hoboken den—and the woman with him! *A blonde woman with a mannish walk . . . broad shoulders and narrow hips, yet with long legs and curves . . . female mannish, the tomboy grown up.* No wonder she'd hidden under the raincoat, man's hat to cover her hair, and dark glasses! The style of a fellow professional. Hired to have Doctor Faith hold me? To stick a signal on my apartment while she searched my office? Everything pointed to it—and she pointed straight at Carl Pike.

I paid for my beer, forgot about dinner. All I needed now was some dates. And some proof.

15

The dead James McBride's house seemed as abandoned as the first time, without light or sound or movement. There was still no answer to my ringing, and the front door was still locked. Yet as I walked around the dark house, I sensed a presence.

There was no pile-up of mail in the letter box, no yellowing newspapers on the overgrown lawn. The soil around the hibiscus and roses wasn't hard and cracked, and there was a car inside the closed and locked garage. On the open rear patio the hanging plants were moist and healthy.

I tried the patio door. It was open.

I stood in a dim, medium-sized living room, neat and orderly, looking in the shadowy light like a thousand middle-class, Middle-Western living rooms I'd seen. Solid and comfortable, without frills, and dirty now, dust thick on the tables, unopened newspapers, mail, empty paper bags littered on the chairs and couches. The center hall and the dining room across it were the same. Dusty, littered with tracked-in leaves and dirt on the carpeting. The stairs up were cluttered at the bottom with bits of clothing, small objects, books that looked like someone had put them there to be taken upstairs and then forgotten them.

I went into the dark kitchen. She was there.

"Mrs. McBride?"

She sat alone, not drinking or doing anything, papers on the table with what looked like lists on them. She hunched her thin shoulders when I spoke, half closed her pale eyes as if the noise, or her name, hurt them like a bright light.

"Can I talk to you?" I said. "About your husband?"

A thin woman who looked in her late thirties, her dirty blonde hair dull and half combed, with a thin face that seemed almost girlish in the soft shadows of the kitchen. She wore a print dress, her shoulder blades jutting against the cloth, the dress stained, the buttons open to show a small, dirty bra, all wrinkled and limp as if she'd slept in the dress.

"Jim's not here." Her voice was light, polite. "I'm sorry."

"I know," I said. "I'd like to ask some questions."

"He's dead," she said. "Jim's dead."

"I'm sorry. When did it happen? The accident?"

She moved restlessly. "You're a friend of Jim's? We don't have many friends. His work keeps him so busy. He loves it."

"No, I never knew him."

"A few colleagues," she said, following her own path, "but they were busy, too. His work and us. It was enough."

"Can you tell me the date he died, Mrs. McBride?"

Her eyes were luminous in the dark. "Mrs. McBride? I suppose I still am. No Mr. McBride, just Mrs. I'm planning our menus, but . . . What do I like to eat? I forget. I buy for Jim, and—" she shook herself—"I must make some plans. The house . . . There's my sister in Denver. Or—"

She was doing more than take it hard. Not quite sane in the dark house, probably hadn't turned on a light for days, weeks. Sleeping in her clothes. The kitchen a mess of dirty dishes, litter. Making unfinished lists, brooding.

"In August," I said. "A little over a month ago."

"You never think he could die. Only forty—"

I realized that she was crying, had been for some time. Silently, the tears rolling down but not changing her voice or manner as if she didn't know she was crying.

"He had two job offers," I said. "Which one had he decided to take?"

She was suddenly aware of her tears, mopped at her face with a dirty dish towel. It brought her into the present, an awareness of me, but with a time lag, like a tape out of synchronization.

"In August, yes, a Wednesday. The fourteenth, I think. I'm not sure. He was there two days. The thirteenth and fourteenth, I think. We buried him on the seventeenth. They all came. Dr. Foley spoke, gave the euology."

"The police were sure it was an accident?"

"I don't know which position he'd decided on. His work. I know he had to accept one, of course."

"Had to?"

"He was disturbed those weeks. In August. Angry, even furious. He called the Titanium Development people, arranged to go up there. On the thirteenth, I'm sure. The thirteenth, you see? He called IMR too, all the way to New York. The day before, I remember. I had to pay the bill . . . later."

"He was disturbed? Why? Did he mention anything, anyone? Carl Pike?"

She looked up quickly, her eyes dark. "Accident? Yes, a horrible accident! He always hated heights. Dizzy. He—" her face went blank. "Yes, he had to accept some position, Dr. Foley couldn't renew his contract. A budget cut, Dr. Foley was very unhappy. He was having to cut back, let Jim and Carl Pike go. He . . . Carl Pike? Why would Carl Pike have made Jim so angry? You think—!"

"Did Pike know Jim was going to Santa Barbara?"

Her answers had caught up to my questions, but now she ran ahead on her own. A motor out of gear—first behind, then ahead. Hearing her own voices.

"Carol, she always pushed him! Saying Jim didn't give Carl enough credit, hating that little house, never satisfied. You think she killed Jim! You do, she or Carl! Oh, they knew he was at Titanium Development! They killed him! They—!"

I tried to slow her. "I didn't say—"

"They said they were at home, but who *saw* them?" She glared at me in the dark kitchen as if I'd said I saw them. "I heard them tell the police—at home that night, the kids away. *Away!* Kids talk, you see? You don't believe Carol was at home. Carl lied for her."

"Why Carol?"

"Carl?" Her luminous stare. "Yes, Carl did it! He got the IMR job. Ruth Montrose here the next day. The next day! Like a vulture, waiting."

She was building it, manic. I tried to calm her.

"We don't know that, but I'll find out. Only we have to be careful, don't let them guess we suspect."

"Find out, yes." She was calmer, eyes bright in the dark. "I have to pull myself together. Get hold of myself, yes."

She got up, began to gather the loose papers on the table. She didn't turn on the light, turned to the sink, and I left her starting to scrape the dishes, put them into the dishwasher in the dark. How much could I trust her? The dates, maybe, not much more. I drove back to 101, turned north again. Maybe the neighbors could tell me more, or maybe I'd find more in the beach cottage. What had that blonde tomboy-grown-up been doing at the cottage? Was Pike out here? Guilt-ridden?

As I climbed up to the cottage, the sound of the surf all around in the night, I saw the car parked behind it, and a light in the living room. Someone who knew how to drive in a back way. I stepped softly to a window. Carol Pike stood in the living room looking around at her old furniture. In a pink blouse and white pants she was close to a lamp, and I could see a yellow lace bra and yellow bikini panties through the thin clothes. The wispy bikini stretched full and lean over a solid body not promised by the cool, Gibson girl image. I went in.

"Short Hills is a lot better," I said.

"Oh!" she jumped. "Mr. Fortune, you startled me. What are you doing here?"

"Investigating," I said.

"I was looking for Carl," she said as if the two things had no connection. "I'm very worried now. He's never been gone this long. I hoped, thought—"

"He might come here? Why? You never liked it."

"We liked it, but it was beneath Carl's potential."

"He's meeting his potential at IMR."

"Yes, he is," she said firmly, but her voice was uneasy.

"But he has troubles," I said. "You know a blonde woman, mannish, about five-eight, a hundred and forty, short skirts."

"No," she said, and shook her head. "Carl isn't here."

"Why would he be? Guilt? Scene of the crime? Except that would be up in Santa Barbara."

"Guilt?" Then she got my meaning, paled. "Stop it, Dan, please. Don't even talk about McBride; it's frightening. Poor Jim's accident was awful. Don't you think I've thought about how his death was our chance? We gain by his tragedy. *The Monkey's Paw* thing, what price will we pay? I'm not superstitious, I'm worried about Carl, but you can't think that he—"

"Then why is he running, hiding? A week and a half."

"He's not hiding."

"Then what is he doing?"

"I . . . I don't know," she said, and her voice dropped. Full and thick. "Dan, please, I—"

Sensual, as if she had something too big inside her. Enticing, but she didn't know how. No, she knew how, but couldn't. I remembered the bikini pants, and in my mind saw that body before her mirror in the brief cloth, the swell and curve barely concealed. Preening, the beautiful body to be admired, but inviolate. Not spoiled by the violation of a male. Grooming herself, but for whom?

"Dan—?"

Certainly not for me. A Weaver, maybe—power and class and status—but not me. So she was trying to turn me away from why Pike was hiding. If I played along, maybe I'd learn why. I took her shoulder in my hand, watched her eyes, said:

"I wonder if there's anything to drink around?"

I felt her imperceptible flinch at my touch, but she smiled:

"I don't know. I'd love something. To relax."

I nodded, squeezed her arm, and went out into the kitchen. The refrigerator wasn't even running, and the cabinets were all empty. She must have known! I went back into the living room. She was gone. I ran for the back door, heard her car start. It was gone before I got outside. I stood in the night, swore.

A hand came over my shoulder, got my wrist. A slim hand. I lunged forward. A mistake. In an instant my arm was twisted behind me, my own movement used against me: judo. If I tried to turn, move at all, the arm could snap like glass.

I didn't move. A hand gripped my neck, squeezed the artery. My ears roared. My knees buckled. I floated . . . and lay with my face against a wooden floor. My arm was still behind me. I tested it. It moved—and so did my feet. I was face-down with my legs and arm trussed together behind me. My mouth was taped.

I felt hands test my bonds, tried to twist and see. All I saw was a pair of bare legs rising smooth to an area of shadow and blue silk cloth. Blue panties under a brief gray skirt. I knew: the blonde from Hoboken again. Electronics, judo and nice legs. Some woman. A pat on my buttocks—pro-to-pro—and silence.

Helpless, I lay listening to the sound of the surf out in the night. I lay there for a long time. The moon rose, my arm and legs grew numb, the night became colder. I thought about the blonde. Who was she, and why was she blocking me? Pike?

Twice I heard voices on the beach, tried to get their attention by kicking over a chair in the cottage. No one came.

Toward midnight I heard singing close. I kicked the wall. A face appeared. A solitary fisherman who freed me. He had some whisky. Warm, I thanked him, gave him the price of a new bottle, and twenty minutes later was in a motel. It was too late to go on. I was tired, sore and shaky.

I went to sleep wondering where the blonde woman fitted.

16

I woke up still wondering, and sure that she had been the woman across the Passaic with the black leader, too. With me almost from the start, but was she protecting Pike or chasing him? Had he hired her, or someone else—protecting or chasing. Somehow, I had a hunch she didn't come as cheap as I did.

I had a quick breakfast, took the twenty-minute drive north to Santa Barbara. It was clear, warm and green in the oasislike city on the coast. Even the ring of mountains were green. In September that wasn't good—the fire season, and too much green on the dry slopes was danger.

But I wasn't thinking about the fire hazard as I left 101 on Santa Barbara Street and drove up to the police station. I was thinking about the short drive from Carl Pike's beach cottage to this city. With plenty of time to push a man off a cliff, an hour round-trip, tops. The detective in charge of the McBride investigation was out. I left my name, said I'd be back.

Titanium Development was a cluster of low buildings perched among trees and brush on the cliffs above the beach halfway to Goleta. When I used McBride's name, the president saw me at once. His name was Sturgis. He had a cluttered desk in a small, busy office, wore a stained laboratory coat, and looked sad.

"A loss, Mr. Fortune, for everyone. For science. I still can't believe it. If only we'd let IMR have him."

"I'm not sure IMR would have gotten him anyway," I said.

"You think he was going to turn them down?" He lit his pipe. "He did seem to like us, and we hoped, but—" A shrug.

"Maybe someone didn't want him to go to IMR," I said.

His pipe hung suspended. "You're joking."

"Was Carl Pike under consideration here too?"

"No, we knew his erratic reputation so we went for McBride. After the accident we contacted Pike, but Ruth Montrose had beaten us." He smoked. "Carl Pike? You're suggesting—?"

"Just wondering," I said. "McBride was here two days?"

"Yes, he came up on the thirteenth, studied our projects and facilities, discussed possibilities with us that night so stayed over at my house. We talked most of the night, and he did seem impressed by the freedom we give our people, our devotion to open research."

"But IMR offered more money?"

"I'm sure they did, a lot more. Still, McBride didn't seem that concerned with the dollars, more with length of contract. He wanted a ten-year contract, time to do long projects."

"Did he talk to anyone else? Make phone calls?"

"Yes, the police checked that. He made a call from my house to IMR, several personal calls. His wife, of course."

"Any to Foley Institute?"

"No, apparently not."

"What did he do on the fourteenth?"

"Went over the details of his new titanium process mostly. He seemed relaxed, even jovial. About seven o'clock, after some drinks but before dinner, he took a walk on our grounds." He shook his head sadly. "I had no idea he was going to take the cliff path, or that he didn't like heights. When he hadn't returned by nine, we went looking for him."

"Can you show me where it happened?"

He nodded, led me out the side of the building. We walked across a ragged, sandy lawn of thick Kikuyu grass, and under oaks and eucalyptus to a narrow trail at the top of the cliffs. The cliffs were steep, a loose, sandy clay. A quarter of a mile from the buildings, Sturgis stopped.

"It was here. The rocks are below, you see?"

They were large rocks close under the clay cliff. A spot where the sea came right up to the cliffs in winter. The path ran right at the edge, there had been a guard rail but it had fallen down the cliff as the land eroded away. The edge of the path was loose, breaking off. A very dangerous spot. There were houses nearby, but the spot itself was hidden by tall brush.

We went back. I thanked Sturgis and drove to the police station. The detective was there, a young one named Reagen.

"If it was murder, it's the perfect kind," he said. "A shove over a cliff. No weapon, no evidence, no witnesses."

"But you thought about it? Not surprised I'm here?"

He was an eager young man. "McBride didn't like heights, why did he go so close to the edge? He'd been drinking, but not so much. The ground was chewed up some at the top, like there could of been a scuffle. He fell farther out than I'd of expected from a slip, and there was no dirt under his fingernails."

"If he'd slipped, he'd have clawed at the dirt?"

He nodded. "But he could of slipped over backwards, and there's a hump in the cliff he might of hit and bounced out. The marks on the dirt could of been made anytime, or even by the land slippage out there."

"No evidence or witnesses at all?"

"We've got witnesses who saw people around the area, but far off, and their descriptions are useless. Just one woman and two men, separate, walking around."

"Size? Clothes? Hair color? Anyone with a beard?"

"None of the descriptions are that good. Not even enough for the artist. They might remember more if we had someone to show them, but that's about it. We did find this on the rocks."

It was a small, brass key. Made on a blank from Master Lock Company, Milwaukee, with a number stamped on it: A1517. But no locksmith name, and it wasn't a door key. A desk, or filing cabinet, or locker, or strong box. Any small spring lock.

"In the rocks a few feet from McBride," Reagen said. "Not there long, the tide would have washed it away or buried it. It isn't McBride's, doesn't fit any locks at Foley Institute or Titanium Development. Anyone could have dropped it."

I didn't ask for a copy. If a killer had dropped it, the lock it fitted would be changed by now. Without a locksmith's name, it could have been made anywhere. Without a suspect to pin a location, there was no hope of tracing it to a maker.

"So you've closed it? Accident?"

"We've left it open a crack. We passed out a call for anyone around the spot at the time. One man came to us, a local. No one else. It bothers me a little. There's two more."

"Yeh," I said. A very slim doubt. People don't answer police calls, or even hear them made.

I took the coast highway south this time. Through Ventura and Oxnard, past the great rock of Pt. Mugu, Zuma Beach, the wall-to-wall houses of Malibu, and into L.A. At L.A. International I had a half hour before a noon flight. I called Emily Hahn at IMR in New York. Only eight-thirty A.M. in New York, but she was there, her voice dull.

"You haven't seen Weaver?" I asked gently.

"No," she said. "What do you want, Dan?"

I didn't take offense, most people have to lick their own wounds in some corner alone. We have to let them.

"What was the date Berger came to California in August? Ruth Montrose, too. You bought the tickets, right?"

"Hold on." She was back after only moments. "Walter went out early on August fourteenth, to Los Angeles. Miss Montrose went on the twelfth, to San Francisco. She had business there."

"Thanks," I said. "I'll call you in New York."

"All right, Dan."

The flight landed at Kennedy just after eight P.M., I got into Manhattan by nine. It was too late to talk to Marie Berger, and I wanted to know everything I could about Carl Pike's actions the last month before I braced her. I unpacked in my bedroom, opened a beer, and called Franklin Weaver. There was no answer. I thought for a time, finished my beer, and looked up Ruth Montrose's Manhattan number. Her cool voice answered, grew cooler when I identified myself.

"I'm not alone, Mr. Fortune. Call me at my off—"

"When Berger went to L.A. in August, was it to meet you?"

There was a silence. "I wasn't aware Walter was in California at that time. If he was, I didn't see him."

"Isn't that peculiar? You're his boss."

"He had his own department, Mr. Fortune. Now—"

"But you were there. In San Francisco and Santa Barbara?"

The silence was even longer. "In San Francisco and Ventura, not in Santa Barbara. What are you fishing for, Mr. Fortune?"

"You reached Carl Pike awful fast after McBride died."

Her voice was dry. "Speed isn't a weakness in our operation. I happened to be in California. We were prepared to make Pike an offer if McBride decided on Titanium Development."

"Had he decided?"

"We never knew."

"Weaver thinks he did, chose Titanium Development."

"Frank was in Europe. I suppose when he heard we'd hired Pike, and of McBride's accident, he assumed McBride had taken Titanium's offer. A logical assumption."

"How did you hear of McBride's death?"

"Foley called New York, my secretary called me."

"Where's Carl Pike now? What's bothering him?"

"I wouldn't know on either. Good-bye, Mr. Fortune."

I took a shower, changed into more comfortable clothes, and went out to get some dinner. Then I walked downtown to Tenth Street. I still wanted to talk to Weaver about Carl Pike. I got an answering buzz at Leslie's apartment, went up. She was waiting in her doorway in a red robe, but not for me. She went inside when she saw me. I closed the door.

"Alone?" I said.

She lit a cigarette, stood looking at a wall.

"What do you want, Dan?"

She looked good—very good. Alive and happy. Involved.

"I think I've got it solved, Leslie," I said. "Carl Pike killed a man out in California, probably a spur-of-the-moment desperation. Walter Berger saw it, or guessed it and had proof. He blackmailed Pike when Pike came to New York. Somehow, maybe chasing around IMR after the lease, Jake found out, cut himself in, and one of them hit him and killed him."

She stared at the wall, smoked her cigarette.

"Blackmail," I said. "Don't you want to know, or did you know all along? Even part of it until Jake got hit?"

"I was worried he might be in some scheme. That was all. I didn't know anything about blackmail."

"And you don't want to hear about it?"

"No, I don't want to hear about it!" Now she turned to me, her eyes angry, in pain, and restless. "He's dead, what does it matter? Can't I have a chance? A winner for once? Frank's strong. I want that power, all of it! I want him, Dan. A winner, some fun, part of the big pie!"

"All right," I said, turned to go.

"Dan? You're sure? Blackmail?"

"It looks like it."

She sat on her couch. "Poor Jake."

That was all, but it carried a world in it. I went out and down—*Poor Jake*: for his short, hard life; for his struggle that failed; for wanting a woman who made him need to succeed too much. Poor Jake, she said on that couch they'd bought for their solid hopes, and I left her staring at her past and her future.

I wasn't tired, and I'd done enough damned work for one day. I found a bar, started drinking Irish. So I'd sleep tonight.

17

The difference between what's supposed to be and what is. The lone businessman, dream and backbone of the country. Except he isn't, the corporations are. The real bone and the power. But Jake Carter had believed what was supposed to be, and when, without power and desperate, temptation came he fell. Poor Jake.

I thought about that all night, didn't sleep, and got up to a low, gray sky and the threat of wind. That storm down in the Atlantic was moving closer, somewhere off Hatteras. By nine A.M. I was moving out of Hoboken again. On the train through the rot of Hoboken, the garbage dump of the Flats, the racial hate of Newark, the black ghetto of East Orange, the slowly decaying old of Maplewood, to the green and white affluence of Short Hills. None of that was supposed to be either, but it was.

By nine forty-five I was ringing Marie Berger's doorbell. I woke her up. Her angry voice told me to go away. I went on ringing.

"I'll call the police!" she called down.

"Call them. I want them to hear my story anyway."

She told me to wait. I waited. Twenty minutes, and when she opened the door, she was all smiles. Her plain face a model of graciousness ushering me into that expensive pastel green room that looked like it had been bought en masse from a museum.

"May I get you some coffee, Mr.—? I'm sorry, I forget?"

I saw where the twenty minutes had gone. She was dressed in an elegant black dress, girdled and groomed—hair fixed, jewels on, makeup in place. Her public image.

"Fortune," I said. "No coffee, no tea, just answers."

Her face turned nasty, she didn't like me. I didn't give a damn. I'd met Walter Berger, I'd heard his history. A quiet man, a plodder. She had the quick, sharp eyes, the mercurial changes. If Berger had become a blackmailer, he hadn't done it on his own.

"You said your husband went to New York to meet Weaver the day before he died. What time did he go. Early?"

She lit a cigarette. "Yes, about five o'clock."

"Weaver talked to him at ten. What else was he doing?"

"I can't really say, can I? I wasn't there."

"When I called, told you he wasn't in his office, you were startled. You hung up fast. Where did you think he was?"

"I had no idea. He was supposed to be in his office."

"No," I said. "He must have been out of his office a hundred times since you married him. But you were worried, you knew he was up to something, and you knew it could be dangerous."

"Really! I don't have to listen to—"

"Yes you do," I said. "You see, I *know*."

She didn't flinch, and she didn't protest. Her face became cool, even cold. Speculative. I heard the outer door open and close, but she didn't look toward it and neither did I.

"On August fourteenth," I said, "Berger went to California. No one seems to know exactly why, and no one who should have seen him out there did. He'd been involved in hiring a Dr. James McBride for IMR. On the evening of the fourteenth, McBride fell off a cliff and died. I think McBride was pushed, Berger saw who did it, and decided to get rich by blackmail."

"Blackmail?" George Engels came into the room, walked toward his sister. She'd obviously called him while I cooled my heels outside. "Walter was tense the last month, nervous. You were keyed up, talking about a world cruise at last. McBride? I know I heard that name in this house. You were always greedy, Marie. Walter wouldn't think of blackmail on his own. No, that's your hand, isn't it? Get rich quick!"

"Crap," she said.

She leaned and put out her cigarette. Calm and cool. One more of her sudden changes, maybe the last.

"Listen good," she said, "I'll only tell it once. Walter told me he had some big, important deal. He didn't say what it was. He said we'd be rich, important. I don't know what he was doing. I didn't know it was dangerous, maybe a crime, until he was killed, and I still don't know what it was."

"Who was he blackmailing, Mrs. Berger?" I said.

"I didn't know he was. I don't know who."

Engels said, "You're lying, Marie. I can see it."

"Walter's dead. If anything was done, he did it alone. Nothing can connect me now. Nothing. Believe me."

I believed her. She would have made sure.

"You don't want his killer caught, the murders solved?"

"And maybe be an accessory? No, I've told my story."

Engels said, "You're a liar, a thief, perhaps an accessory to murder, and you see nothing wrong, do you, Marie?"

She looked at him. "You're a hardware store in Millburn, George. Not even in Short Hills. You'll always own a hardware store in Millburn."

"Yes," he said, "thank God."

Her eyes flashed, but only for a second. "You can leave with Fortune. Right now. I've got papers to sign."

We left. Engels offered me a ride to the station.

"She really sees nothing wrong, you know?" he said. "Get all you can, any way you can. What's right is what you can get away with. She's not alone these days."

"No," I said, "but she didn't get away with much now."

"Enough, I expect. Insurance, his pension. She's not just thinking of safety. Talking could make trouble about those."

"Yeh," I said as we arrived. "Thanks, Engels."

"Is there anything bad about owning a hardware store, Mr. Fortune?"

"Nothing at all," I said.

"No," he said.

He drove off. Ten minutes later the train came.

At Weaver's Park Avenue building the doorman opened the door for me this time. There had been enough police going in and out. He didn't even call up when I flashed my license, and I rode to Weaver's private landing. The same woman's voice answered. I identified myself, asked for Weaver. The door opened.

"He's not here, Mr. Fortune," Leonore Weaver said. "I don't know where he is."

She wore green slacks and a pale green blouse this time, walked into the large, rich, tasteful living room, lit a cigarette, and forgot to offer me one. Not herself, tense.

"No," she said, turned on me. "I know where he is, and I expect you do too. Carter. An Armenian this time. Exotic."

Her voice, her whole manner, was brittle. The slacks did less for her than even the red evening dress had. Too big and soft for slacks. Too much hip and too little breast, comfortable not chic, a matron at home. Her soft, routine face under rigid control, but the finishing school voice on the edge of crying.

"I'm sorry," I said, looked at the green slacks. "Has he known her long?"

"Long? Aren't you her friend? I understood you practically introduced them? Oh, Frank doesn't hide his women from me. Not from anyone."

"I wondered if he'd known Leslie before," I said.

"Leslie. What a nice name. Is she beautiful?"

"Yes. You went out the night I was here. You didn't happen to follow your husband later, did you? To a parking lot near IMR Center? Came home first, changed your clothes?"

"Why would I follow him? He always tells me."

"That doesn't mean you like it," I said.

"Anyway, he was home that night." The faint bitterness I'd heard earlier wasn't faint now. "Why shouldn't I like it? I'm his wife, his family, his home. I have my role, I'm needed. He loves me, he says so." But a bitterness mixed with unhappiness, loss. "I love him, you see? I do. And I'm jealous. Of all of them. Of IMR. That's his real woman, father and country."

She was almost crying now, but not quite. Refusing to cry, calling up all her training in those good, well-bred schools.

"Mrs. Weaver, did he ever mention a McBride, or Carl Pike?"

"What? Oh, yes, he hired Carl Pike. Or Ruth Montrose did. He said they'd wanted a better man, but something went wrong, and Ruth Montrose told him that Pike was as good. Frank was very upset at the time. He seemed to think Ruth had made a mess of it somehow." The tears in her voice again. "Even Ruth, he had to—" She took a deep breath. "My, Frank would say I'm making an unholy spectacle of myself. Forgive me. It passes."

"Why should it pass?" I said.

Chronic misery is like that storm down in the Atlantic—it has violences and calms. She sank into a sudden calm. Or maybe it was my implied criticism of Weaver. She rose to his defense.

"It's not that he doesn't love me," she said. "One woman simply isn't enough for his needs. Too much restless power, too intense. Women are *there* for him, part of his world. His world to manage, control, rule and have. Part of what he is."

"As good an excuse as any," I said.

"No, it's not an excuse. It's true. Women are as natural for Frank as being an executive. I feel bitter, I blame him, but I know I'm wrong. I knew what he was before we married. Women have a way of forgetting that they knew, and blame a man for being himself, for not changing for their sake."

"Men do it too, Mrs. Weaver," I said. "Call it human."

But she was thinking. "For great men a wife and family is only an incident in their lives. Not really of central importance. Necessary, but not vital. That is only themselves, their purpose. Great men have a strong sense of self. Something I never had. A sense of complete identity, of ego."

She thought about that, and so did I. I knew what she meant, I don't have that sense of self either. It makes losers. She must have had the same thought, and I watched the violence of her storm rise up in her again. Her eyes dark, stiff.

"But wives are necessary, too. To entertain the guests, give the parties. And, of course, to be there when he needs a woman and the others aren't on hand. I suppose some wives have husbands who bother them all the time. They'd probably think I was fortunate. Do you bother your wife, Mr. Fortune? A lot?"

She was flirting, and she didn't know how either. I was getting tired of women with suggestions they didn't mean.

"No wife," I said. "Give him trouble. It might help."

I headed for the door. She seemed shocked. She probably thought men never refused a hint. What else would she think?

On Park Avenue the low afternoon sky was dark, a few raindrops falling, the wind rising, and I still wanted Weaver. I called his office. He was out. I got a taxi.

The Mercedes wasn't on Tenth Street. I rang Leslie's bell anyway, and when she took a time to answer, knew she wasn't alone.

Weaver sat on the clean, worn couch like a prime minister in the servants' quarters, but Leslie didn't look like the servant. In a new, white, two-piece evening jump suit, she looked like the queen herself. The silky pants, tight over her hips and belly, flared wide at the ankle above white sandals. Bare in the middle, the top was fitted over those breasts, high at the neck, and puffed into short sleeves. Her dark eyes were confident. Weaver had his hands full and he knew it. Knew it and liked it. They were together. Leslie arched her back, provoking.

"Hello, Dan. Have a drink, join us," she said.

If Weaver was annoyed, he hid it beautifully. He wanted her, I saw that. Wanted and admired. Who knew, maybe Leslie was the one who would handle him. He read my mind again.

"Join us, Dan. Here, I take orders."

"Without the tank or the army?" I said.

"There are times when they're in the way," he grinned.

Leslie got me the drink, a beer. She wanted him.

"Leslie told you what I think?" I asked.

"About Berger and Carl Pike? Yes, but I think you're wrong."

"Then what was Berger doing in town? Pike was in town too. Drunk, wandering. Both at the lot. Where did you call Berger?"

"I don't know what he was doing," Weaver admitted. "In New York, but not at the office. That wasn't like Walter, I agree. But . . . I called him at the Cambridge Hotel. He used it."

"How did you know he was there?"

"I didn't. I called his home, got no answer."

Where had Marie Berger been? She hadn't mentioned going out that night. A mistake? Or had Berger been expendable?

"Why am I wrong?" I asked.

"I don't know, I admit it. But men like Carl Pike don't murder for a job. He's good, Dan, could have had many jobs."

"Why didn't he then?"

"I don't know. Unless . . . Carol likes the top, eh?"

"Had McBride decided to come with IMR or not?"

"I thought he'd turned us down, but Ruth Montrose says I'm wrong. She called me about it today. Perhaps he hadn't."

"Even if he had," I said, "Pike didn't know. McBride only called IMR from Santa Barbara. Who did he talk to here at IMR?"

Weaver was uneasy. "I can't find out. No one knows."

"Walter Berger? Berger *knew* his decision, and that's why he hurried out? To sign up McBride, but saw a murder instead. That would explain everything just about perfectly."

"Yes," Weaver said, "it would. Especially why Berger went."

"But not Carl Pike? Then who? Ruth Montrose?"

"Impossible!"

"Carol Pike? You? Nugent? Leslie? Mrs. McBride?"

Leslie had been sitting there in silence, drinking slowly, listening like some large white cat sure of what was to come soon. She had the same power Weaver did. A sense of self. Of her needs.

"I don't even know how to get to Santa Barbara," she said.

"I'll have to take you," Weaver said. "There's a ranch, the San Ysidro. Cottages in the hills, close but isolated."

"When?" she said.

This time they didn't have to tell me to go, or even hint. I wasn't there. Not for her, and not for him. Especially not for him. I left.

On the street the wind blew me against a small tree, and I saw her. Emily Hahn. She stood across the street in the light, blowing rain, looking up at Leslie's building. I went to her.

"He's up there, isn't he?" she said.

"Yes. How about a drink? Coffee? Some talk?"

"All right," she said. "Come to my place."

I took her arm. In heels she was taller than I am, much taller, but she clung to me. I hailed a taxi.

18

Her enormous room with its gay, irreverent posters and floppy furniture was cold and forlorn, dulled by the dark sky outside and a bare neatness as if she'd spent nights alone cleaning out the room. She plugged in a small electric heater.

"Get out of that wet jacket, make coffee. I'll change."

I found the coffee in the tiny kitchenette, made a large pot, set it perking, and stripped off my jacket. I warmed up over the electric heater. She came from the bathroom wearing the voluminous purple robe, sat on the floor close to the heater. I let her sit, her chin resting on her covered knees, staring at the glowing heater as if it were an open fire. Warmth, and the sound and aroma of the perking coffee began to fill the room.

"I don't blame her so much," she said. "She's alone, it must have been terrible for her. Just knocked down like that, and then dying before they could even talk again, without even seeing each other again." She shivered. "Mr. Carter, Walter Berger, that Dr. McBride. Do you or the police know yet?"

"It looks like Berger was blackmailing Carl Pike for killing McBride. Jake Carter got caught in the middle. Weaver just helped fill in a missing piece—why Berger went to the Coast so suddenly. It looks like Carl Pike. I don't need much more. A witness, a clue. Once you know, the clues fall into place."

She nodded, an absent nod. "I don't really blame Frank, either. He never lied or cheated. It's the way he is. I guess if he wasn't like that, he wouldn't be Frank Weaver."

When you're young, it's hard to think much about other people's trouble when you have your own. When you're old too.

"Why do women defend him?" I asked. "All of them."

She thought. "I guess because we know inside that whatever happened was *our* fault. What he is was what attracted us. Dynamic, strong, certain of his values, romantic. His values are different from ordinary men, the kind a girl expects to marry, and that's what intrigued us. I guess it's always clear that we *want* him to make love to us, and if we blame him later, then we were just stupid."

"How are his values different?"

"Most boys, men, you meet need you. You fill their need, as well as them filling yours. Frank doesn't need you, or anyone. He's like IMR itself. No one's indispensable to IMR, it goes on in itself, and no one's indispensable to Frank. You know he'll go on doing his work, what matters. It's kind of simple for a woman, uncomplicated."

"Do women like a simple relation?"

"Sometimes, I guess. All of us. It's peaceful."

"But thin," I said. "Complications make life thick, I think, full. Too simple is kind of empty. No overtones."

She smiled at me. "Well, it's her turn now, I've had mine. I won't try to hold him, or start again. The secretary and the boss, standard. I'll have to start thinking now about what I really want to do. Some better work."

"You should. You're too good for a secretary, even his."

"Am I?"

"Yes," I said, and I stood, went to her, sat down on the floor beside her, and kissed her. I wanted to.

She responded slowly at first and then held to me and her young lips held tight. I pulled her close to me, and knew that she was naked under the big, heavy robe. For me this time? I found her body under the thick cloth. She didn't pull away at once, but very gently, being careful not to make me feel she didn't want my hand on her. But she did pull away, huddled close to herself under the robe, stared at the glowing heater.

"I think it's hard," she said, "for other men to understand his fascination, Frank's. It's his world, partly, the importance, and how good he is in it, his ability. He commands his world. He's really a fine man, Dan, strong and honest. Daring. You know, I really adored him. A great man, and a nice man. My only man."

She gave a little shiver under the robe. Like a muscle spasm, and a shaking away at the same time. "My first man, and my only man. I waited much too long. Stupid. Then I picked Frank to be the one. Afraid of complications, perhaps. But—" She sat silent, and then she looked at me. "But I want another man. Not Frank, not now. Another man, Dan. I want you."

She responded at once when I kissed her this time, held me tight when I touched her, and her nakedness was for me. A big girl, warm from the heavy robe, full and pale and filling the big bed on the bright Arabian cover.

After some time I unplugged the heater, turned out the lights, and went back to her on the big bed in the dark, gray afternoon light that didn't seem so very dark or gray anymore.

"Ummmmmmmm," she nestled against my neck, her lips warm.

"I wish I were a simple man," I said. "I'm not. I want to stay a while. A long while."

"Can we go somewhere? I've got vacation time. I never wanted to take vacation time."

"California? Santa Barbara, maybe. Stay there."

She rubbed against me, slowly. "You've got work."

"No I don't, it doesn't own me. No work is indispensable. One detective isn't important to the world."

"But he is to me, I like him, and I like how he does his work," she said. "I like it that he helps people."

"It may take a while. I think I've got the answer, but I can't prove it. Pike could even be dead somewhere. If he is, we'll probably never be sure."

"Suicide? No, I don't think so, Dan. Not Pike."

"Then where? Would Weaver protect him?"

"I don't think so, but—?"

"He might? Or Ruth Montrose might?"

She kissed me. "Find out, Dan, and then come back."

She wanted me to work—and she wanted to be alone. Not so simple a relation. I felt that inside—for me, and maybe for her. She was young, I wasn't. She wanted time. All right.

I dressed. I'd give her the time. I left her there under the Arabian cover, curled up, thinking of Frank Weaver, yes, but maybe of me too. It was time to call Gazzo, report.

I went up the rickety stairs to my office, thinking for the first time in almost two weeks that I wasn't going to have it for long. I'd almost forgotten they were tearing it down. Work is the healer of many things. Now I remembered, and it depressed me, and I thought of Marty, and that depressed me. Or maybe it was just that I was more than halfway from forty to fifty, and she wasn't yet thirty.

My door was open.

I stepped lightly along the corridor. For the second time in two weeks I wished I had my gun. I listened. Someone coughed in my office. A rasping, dry cough, and shifted in a chair, and spoke low to someone. To himself! A man talking to himself. I pushed open the door.

"You don't do much work, do you?" he said irritably.

Old Ben Maddox sat stiffly in my extra chair, his cane close to his bony hand. His skeletal face dared me to say I worked. I sat down behind my desk.

"Where the hell have you been?"

"Mindin' my own business," he snapped. "Whyn't you try it? Puttin' the cops to huntin' and houndin' me!"

"You were at the parking lot, and you ran. Why?"

"I got a right to go where I likes."

I reached for my phone. "Maybe you'll tell the police."

"No!" His emaciated face was yellow, afraid of the police. "That's why I come, the cops've been houndin' me all over everywhere. You put 'em after me, ain't nowhere I can go. Anyway, I want to go home. So I come to tell you."

His voice was almost plaintive when he said "home." I knew his "home," and the way he said the word told a whole story of age and loneliness. A life so desolate that he saw that cold, barren apartment as "home," wanted to go there as to a green and pleasant land. His place.

"Why did you hide? Run off?"

"So I wouldn't have to do nothin' to help *him*. Jake Carter was a liar! A dirty-mouthed blasphemer! The guy killed him did good. I wasn't tellin' anythin' to help that Jake."

A mean, stubborn old man taking his revenge. A moment of triumph, of power, in his nothing life.

"What did you come to tell, Maddox?"

He squirmed. "I was in my back window, around nine-thirty. I heard this ruckus in that office shack. Shoutin', 'n a fight. No one else was around. So I went down to the yard to see better, you know? I see Jake Carter come runnin' from the shack with somethin' in his hand, catch up to someone near the fence. They was behind the fence, but then I see Carter go down flat in the openin' like he been hit by an ax. He just lay there. Someone just walked off, 'n after a while I took a closer look."

"You didn't get help?"

"I saw he was hurt bad, 'n I was glad! He got what was comin' to him. I just hung around watchin' until you come 'n found him. Then you chased me, but you didn't catch me."

"You didn't see who hit him?"

"Sure I did. Right near that shack in the light. That guy with the beard was there before when those punk kids bothered my dogs. Same guy, I remembered his clothes. Later on I saw a woman, too. Big woman in green pants like a man. The way they dresses nowadays! Tall woman, big all over."

"A blonde woman?"

"Didn't see her hair, too dark 'n blue light on the fence."

It didn't matter. Carl Pike had left the lot at midnight. Up until now it hadn't seemed logical that he'd have stayed at the lot so long if he'd hit Jake Carter. But he had. I still didn't know why he had, but now a witness placed him right there when Jake Carter was hit. It just about closed the door.

"Get out of here, Maddox," I said. "Go home, enjoy your revenge while you can. The police are going to want to talk to you about not reporting the fight or getting help."

Sallow, he got up viciously. He wanted to savor his revenge, but the police scared him. He limped out sideways on his cane like some old crab, and I heard him clumping slowly down the stairs. He might have been as responsible for Jake Carter's death as anyone, but my threat was hollow. The police would give him a scare and a lecture, no more. If they tried to prosecute everyone who failed to help or report, there wouldn't be enough jails anywhere.

I called Gazzo, told him all of it from California to Ben Maddox. He took it all down, names and dates. He'd check.

"I guess that's it," he said. "We'll find Pike."

After I hung up, I sat there for some time. The rain was heavier outside now, the wind steadily rising. Night soon, the storm building to a big one, and the case just about out of my hands. Finding Carl Pike was all that was left, and that was a job for the police. They had the tools and the time. If I had any small doubts and questions, they would wait until Carl Pike could answer them. If he was still alive.

Out of my hands, and I could find a new office, it wasn't the end of the world. I went out in the rain and got some dinner. Then I took a taxi up to East Seventy-seventh and Third. Emily was there, waiting for me. It felt very good.

In the dark later, the rain blowing against the windows, I told her about Pike and what Maddox had seen. She was sad. I said we'd take a trip. She felt better, lay close against me. I didn't care how young she was, or how old I was. I had her.

And all at once I realized that Marty was over. Gone. My long wound-licking was over. Marty, her sharp memory, slipped away like a dream. I wouldn't cry over Marty again, carry her with me, stand in dark doorways thinking about my loss. I'd remember her, a one-time friend, without the ache.

Sooner or later we forget. We can't help it, no matter how long and hard we try not to. It didn't make me feel glad.

The horror, the pain, isn't that we don't forget our loves, but that we do. That to forget, no matter how much we loved, is inevitable.

We forget and go on. I had a new love, and plenty of time.

19

One of the excitements of a new woman, or a new man, is that all your dreams and stories are new again. Time seems so full. Through that night, the rain sometimes hard outside, and sometimes light, she told me her dreams and I told her mine.

"You have more and better," I said. "You're young."

"Why do you talk about age so much, Dan?"

"Because time changes everything," I said. "Go on, tell me everything you want, everything you're going to do."

I lay watching the night shadows play across her full body, and listening as she talked. After a time I noticed that all her plans and visions placed a man beside her. They stood on Adriatic balconies, climbed Alps hand in hand, sailed the Pacific side by side. They had drinks on the patio while the children played. There seemed to be a lot of money, and a lot of time, and he was always there—handsome, devoted, adoring her.

"But what are you going to do?" I asked.

"We'll think of things. Good things," she said, kissed me.

"Not us," I said, "you. What do you want to do, be?"

"Be?" She stroked my chest. "Funny, Frank never asked me that, not once. I'm not sure. I'll have to think. You'll help."

"If I can," I said. "I haven't done too well with myself."

"Good, I'm tired of important men. We won't be important, just rich. Have fun. Make love to me."

Toward morning, after we'd slept a little, she asked how I'd lost my arm. I told her about the Chelsea kid bandit and the fall into the hold of the Dutch ship. She comforted me again.

Somewhere around eight A.M., the rain stopped and a thin sun washing through the fast-moving clouds, we decided on a slow drive to California. The telephone changed that. A call for me. Automatically, I'd left the number where I could be reached.

"Dan?" Carol Pike said from the other end, her voice low and urgent. "I'm sorry, but . . . Dan, he called me! Carl! He's all right, he wants to talk to me."

"Tell him to come in, go to the police. Right now."

"He didn't do anything!" she cried, and I heard her breathing. "Dan, if the police find him . . . He must have an explanation. Come with me, talk to him, hear him. If I'm wrong—"

"All right," I said. "Where are you?"

The police just might be trigger-happy, especially if they surprised him, and somewhere in the back of my mind there was still a doubt, some small thing I'd heard that didn't seem right. And, in a way, Carl Pike was my responsibility.

"In Short Hills. Frank Weaver is coming, too. He said if you agreed to go he'd pick you up at your office."

I explained it to Emily, and she watched me dress. I kissed her, and she gave me a key. I said I'd be back as soon as I could. I left her propped up in bed looking out at the fast-moving sky, and got a cab down on Third Avenue. As I rode downtown, I thought about her hopes. Somehow, they didn't fit me too well. Then, we'd just begun.

In my office I got my gun this time, slipped it into my raincoat pocket, and went down to the street. It wasn't raining, but a wet wind was blowing hard gusts. The black Mercedes drove up half an hour later, and I got in. Except for the chauffeur, Weaver was alone. We headed for the tunnel.

"Where's the army?" I asked.

"Nugent's day off. I was in Connecticut."

"Showing Leslie the pad, or mending fences with the wife?"

His drooping eyelid raised. "Throwing stones, Dan? Carol Pike called me after she spoke to you. How is our Emily?"

"Does it bother you?"

"Of course it does," he said, "but I can't object, can I?"

We came out of the tunnel onto Route 22 through Newark and past the airport, and his mind wasn't on Emily, or Leslie, or any woman. His lean, lined face, older than its years, was worried, and as far as I'd seen, International Metals & Refining was all he really worried about. He liked other things, was concerned with other things, even needed other things, but he never worried about anything but IMR. That's how a man gets to be executive vice president at thirty-seven.

"I think you're wrong, Dan, you know that," he said, looking out at the Flats but not seeing them. "I'm coming along to be sure he gets an honest, complete, fair chance to speak."

"You think I wouldn't give him that?"

"I think you'd mean to, but . . . What real proof is there?"

"We've placed him where Carter was hit, and when. He had the opportunity to kill Berger. Once we place him where McBride fell, at the right time, we've got evidence that should do it."

"I see," he said, thoughtful. "And IMR was the motive?"

"You're paying him a lot more than Foley, right?"

"A lot more, and not for much yet," he said dryly. "He'll get our help and protection, Dan. The best we can buy. Innocent or guilty, I'll not lose a top man without a fight. IMR needs his mind, I won't see it wasted. I'll save him, no matter what."

"Save him," I said. "I solve cases, what happens after I don't control. But I don't like murderers free, Frank."

He shook his head. "That doesn't concern me. McBride is dead, it would be a bad mistake to lose both of them."

"Maybe, but let's find him first, then talk about him."

He nodded. "You'd be a good executive, to the point."

"No I wouldn't," I said. "I like to be free."

He laughed. "Freedom is relative, Dan. A boss has most."

Carol Pike was waiting in that living room full of French Provincial furniture so far from the beach at Ventura. She wore a trench coat, slacks, brimmed felt hat, and was grim. Neither "chaste" nor sensual, only determined. The boy and girl I'd last seen listening to Pike tell of *tee-hees* and *hee-glubs* were with a baby sitter. Carol Pike hurried us out.

As the chauffeur drove east it began to rain heavily, and by the time we turned south on the Garden State Parkway, the wind was whipping broad sheets of water. A tropical storm now, the cars crawling on the Parkway. Except us. Weaver's chauffeur didn't seem to be aware of any storm.

"It's a hotel on the shore," Carol Pike explained. "Near Toms River, run by an old school friend of Carl's. It's closed for the season, on an isolated inlet. That's why he hasn't been found. Skinner's Hotel."

The wind almost blew us off the bridge over the Raritan, and then we were through Eatontown, past Asbury Park and Lakewood, and into Toms River. A gas station man told us how to get to Skinner's Hotel, but shook his head at the storm.

"Ain't safe out there in this. Closed anyway."

Weaver only nodded to the chauffeur, and went. On back roads around and across small rivers and inlets swirled by the wind, and out to the shore of Barnegat Bay. Signs, leaning half over, pointed us across two concrete and one narrow wooden bridge to a big, brown frame hotel from the last century. It stood on a point, but on the leeward side sheltered from the wind scouring everywhere else on the wide, bleak bay. Smoke blew from its chimney. We pulled up in its shelter. No one came to meet us.

The wind blew so violent that it seemed all the water would be blown from the bay leaving a wide, empty hole. A hurricane now. The silent chauffeur and Weaver helped Carol Pike, all three bent and staggering, and I went ahead to find the door.

Something slapped my shoulder, turned me around. I staggered. A hissing whine in my ears. Not the wind. I held to a pole. Only then, delayed by the wind, did I hear the shots.

Someone was shooting at me.

A wood chip flew from the post, brushed my cheek.

I went down flat.

Carol Pike and the chauffeur were down. Weaver was half down, kneeling and staring toward the hotel.

Everything was silent in the violent noise of the wind. Only the wind—without voices or human noise—and the shots.

Two more, faint and blown away. Another, and this time I heard its direction—not from the hotel! From out in the reeds and marsh and blowing curtain of rain.

"Inside!" I yelled as loud as I could. It was like trying to run up a steep, endless cliff. "Inside!" I waved at them, turned, and ran for the first door I could see.

Mud spouted at my feet. A rifle, its aim spoiled by the violent wind, the blinding wall of driven rain, and I made the door just as it opened. The others piled in after me, the chauffeur closing the door like a man pushing against a wall.

"Who the hell are you people? We're closed."

A short, balding man stood in the seashore-style hotel lobby. There was a high ceiling with wooden fan blades that turned slowly as wind seeped through cracks, rattan settees and chairs, dusty Oriental pattern rugs on bare floor, and a long mahogany registration desk. The dining room opened to the left, chairs now piled on bare tables, and a cocktail lounge was to the right with an open fire burning. The hotel was oddly quiet after the hurricane of wind and rain. Stairs led up at the rear on both sides of the desk. A thin young woman was cleaning the stairs, didn't look up. Carl Pike stood in the entrance to the cocktail lounge.

"It's all right, Andy," he said, "I asked them to come."

"Hell of a time to come calling," the bald man said. "If they get stuck here, they'll have to make up their own rooms. I guess we've got enough food." He smiled then. "Except I guess you'd all like a drink more. Go into the bar, I'll scare up some dry clothes."

Neither he, nor the girl, nor Pike was wet. Obviously they hadn't heard the shots over the storm, thought we'd all been blown down. Pike turned and went back into the cocktail lounge without speaking again. We followed him.

"They were shots?" Weaver said in a low voice. "Outside."

"Rifle," I said. "Not from the hotel, from the marsh. And no one in here, someone else."

"Who would shoot at us out here? Why?"

"Not us," I said, "me. Who knows we're here?"

"No one," Weaver said, definite.

"Then it must be someone who knows Pike is," I said.

In the lounge Carl Pike sat at the bar. He had the bottle of whisky near his glass, wore old fishing-type clothes, and his beard was ragged. His pale blue eyes looked at his wife.

"You couldn't come alone, could you? Just us, together."

"Carl, please—" Carol Pike began.

"No, you had to bring *him*." He nodded at Weaver. "The satrap with the gold. IMR, the big time."

"We have a stake in you, Carl, I'm sorry," Weaver said. "We have to know. Did you—?"

"Hold it," I snapped. "Pike, why were you in New York at Jake Carter's parking lot the day I met you?"

Weaver glanced at Carol Pike, but he said nothing. He knew what I was doing. I wanted answers before I told Pike why, made any revelations or accusations. Pike looked at me.

"Fortune, isn't it? You look better than the last time I saw you. What happened in Hoboken? Were you sick?"

"You don't know what happened to me?"

"Me?" He blinked. "Why would I know? We'd barely met."

"Why were you in New York that day? Not at work?"

He shrugged, drank. "I went to talk to Weaver there. That's what I did, sure. Lay it on the line. But I couldn't, so I got drunk, then walked around thinking. I've been walking around thinking ever since. Thinking and drinking. I drink well."

"You were at the parking lot at midnight, to get your car," I said. "But you were there at nine-thirty, too."

He poured more whisky. "I was looking for Jake. Someone to drink with, talk to. Someone out of the high-rent tycoon level. But he wasn't in the office, so I went around the bars to find him. I didn't, so got my car. Never did find old Jake."

"You could have hit him, killed him, and still gone around the bars."

"Killed him?"

"Him and Walter Berger. Or maybe Berger killed Jake, but you killed Berger. Tell us where you were later that night?"

"Berger? What the hell are you talking about? Kill? Me?"

"You," I said. "You killed James McBride out in Santa Barbara. Berger saw you, so you had to kill him. Blackmail."

He put his glass down. We all watched him, the wind shaking the old hotel. He shook his head as if to clear a fog.

"I killed Jim? You mean that accident? Why would I ever have done anything like that?"

"Because McBride had decided to take the IMR job, or you thought so. You wanted the IMR job. An assistant, living in a small beach cottage with secondhand furniture, only part-time—"

He began to laugh. A rising laugh, half crazy.

"Carl!" Carol Pike said, low and angry.

He went on laughing, shook his head at me. "Jim McBride's death was the worst thing that ever happened to me, Fortune."

20

"The worst thing that could have happened," he laughed, "and you think I killed Jim McBride!"

"It was bad for you?" I said. "Why?"

"Because I'm weak." The laugh turned bitter. "When Jim died, IMR needed *me*. I couldn't say no, could I, Carol?"

"We talked it out, Carl," she said. "You know that."

"Did we? Did you listen to me?"

"Of course I did, dear. It was best for all of us." Carol Pike smiled. "No one could turn down such an offer."

"No? I think Fortune there could have."

Carol Pike looked at me as if that was no answer at all, my kind didn't count. Everything I'd seen and heard did a somersault. Sometimes, what things add up to depends on what end of the glass you look at them through. I'd been looking through the wrong end. The facts were the same, they just added to a different answer.

"You *wanted* to work only part-time," I said. "You want to do private research in the garage. You liked that beach cottage and the second-hand furniture."

"Crazy?" Pike said, drank. "The independent scientist, pursuing truth where my interest took me. Where I wanted to look, not where I was told and paid to look. Research *I* found exciting, work worth doing."

"You didn't make enough money," Carol Pike snapped. "We couldn't go on."

"Enough money for who?" Pike said.

"You can still do your private research," she said.

Pike smiled at Weaver. "Can I, Weaver? Anything I want?"

"I don't fence," Weaver said bluntly. "We expect your research to be relevant to IMR's future."

Carol Pike tossed her head. "Then work weekends! Madame Curie did, didn't she? Make your earth-shaking discoveries on the side, you've got a family!"

"I was supporting them, Carol," Pike said.

I said, "Why not some university?"

"They're as bad—government grants, underwritten projects. At least, I thought so. Too late now," he said. "Carol's right, I didn't make much money. No grants, no subsidies, few clients. Some small companies let me do a few projects, not enough. Some salable discovery would have helped, but I never made one like that. The titanium process isn't salable in itself, not yet."

"Then quit," Carol Pike said. "Make me a drink, and tell Frank you quit! Go ahead."

"Quit?" Pike said. He got a glass from under the bar, made her a Scotch and water. Weaver and I shook our heads. He poured more for himself, but he wasn't drunk.

"You thought I was hiding out of guilt, when I was hiding from IMR. Trying to understand why I let it happen, took the job."

"We had no choice, Carl," Carol Pike said.

"We always lived. We didn't have to live in Short Hills."

"All right," she said, "I'm getting angry. This doesn't have to be discussed here and now. I'm going to find some dry clothes, and then we'll go home."

She drained her glass, walked from the lounge toward the thin woman still cleaning the stairs. It was hard to realize that it wasn't noon yet, as dark as night out in the storm.

"She needs security," Pike said. "Security and freedom don't go together. Not in any society, at any time, in any place." He drank. "And her idea of security is other people's idea of luxury."

"Why not?" Weaver said. "It's there to have."

Pike nodded. "The real secret of success. You have to want what success brings—the rewards and the power."

"Part of it," Weaver said. "Mostly it's knowing what's really important, and that you can do the job best."

I said, "Why take the job at Foley? Even part-time?"

"Compromise. One of a long series." Pike shrugged. "That first small step and it gets bigger and bigger. I fought the system all my life, tried to avoid being a cog in some IMR's wheel, a man who does what IMR wants in return for all the comfortable benefits and peaceful security. But it's a powerful system, it needs us to serve it and feed it by consuming, and it's almost impossible to escape without help. Even then, you better be ready to risk disaster, give up a lot."

I knew what he meant. In a way, I'd fought the same fight, and I'd given up a lot. One of the few things I was proud of, took pleasure in, was that I'd never worked for a corporation, big or small, never run for the 7:10 train every day, never done work I didn't want to at the moment. To show for it—a middle-aged roustabout in five cheap, rented rooms, a one-window office they were going to tear down, no pension or paid vacations, and about three hundred dollars in the bank.

"I couldn't give up enough," he said. "Not women. I can't live without a woman. Funny, because I can't handle women, either. I got married. I don't blame Carol, it would have been some woman. Somehow, I want the wrong women. I needed a woman who'd care for *me* so much she'd deny herself, a woman I was vital to. But I'm always attracted to self-centered women, the kind with a strong ego, strong needs and plans. That probably says more about me than about them."

Weaver lit a cigarette, walked to the window, stood looking out at the violent storm laying the reeds flat. Tall and rigid, disgust in every inch of his athletic body.

"The first year we were married," Pike said, "I took a small job so we could go on a vacation, compromised my own work. After that it never stopped, one small, logical step after another, until half-time at Foley, and then IMR. For a house, two cars, the children, a 'decent' life, and now a rich life. To Carol, it's all only right, as it should be. To her a man's only duty is to his wife and family, that's what he exists for. Not for his work, his visions, science, the world."

Weaver turned, scornful. "Of course he does. That's her world, she fights for it the way she should. It's up to *you* to fight for your vision, what you believe, want."

"I never believed in the adversary system of marriage."

Weaver turned back to the window. "You're a fool, Pike."

"If I fight her, I'll lose her!" Pike cried, drank, the liquor having no effect anymore. "Two weeks I've been trying to do it, make the break. I've taken a step, but . . . I can't work for IMR, but if I quit . . . Weakness is a habit, I said that before, didn't I? You know why I took the job? Because I couldn't *guarantee* our future in Ventura."

I said, "To live you have to risk, Pike."

That's true, but it's not so easy to live with. I had help. I lost my arm. It made me different, an outsider. Easier.

"Risk? Yes, but nature gave men a dirty deal. Not just me," Pike said, laughed now. "The tyranny of sex. The most destructive force against a man doing anything in this world is his need of a woman. The most destructive force against a woman doing anything important is her need of children. The force against their doing anything together is the difference in those needs. Men want women, women want children." He shrugged, took a drink. "Nature's way of assuring enough children back when we needed a lot of them to survive. Today we don't need so many, but the instinct is still there, and it plays hell."

Weaver turned again. "A man, and a woman, has to control those needs, Pike, not be controlled by them. That's one of the measures of ability. It's one reason more men than women do big things. The need for children is harder to control."

I remembered what Leonore Weaver had said. Women were only an incident to Weaver, to any great man. Not to Carl Pike.

"Yes, children," Pike said. "Maybe I could quit, make the break, but the children? The mistakes of a marriage don't hurt just the man and the woman, they hurt the kids, too. We mortgage their lives. They have a right to strong, happy parents."

"You'll never break, Pike," Weaver said from the window, still looking out at the storm as if he felt close to it, admired its power. "You make too many excuses, create your own barriers. You don't want to be free, a liar to yourself. Fortune there, I respect him. But you build your own straw men to block you."

"No! I love Carol, don't you see? I don't want to break *from* her, I want to break *with* her. I want us to live free, but together. Both of us. Peaceful, a quiet life. My work *and* her. Why not? A quality life, not quantity. Why can't we live without IMR *or* an endless struggle?"

"Because IMR doesn't want you to," I said.

"Not IMR," Weaver said, "the country. Your way is counterproductive, Pike. Useless. It's childish."

Pike drank, stared at his glass. The whisky was having no effect at all. I watched him. Was it all true? Or only part of it? A clever cover-up? True up to a point, maybe to a month ago? A man can change, both himself and his needs. I watched him as Carol Pike returned in an old dress that was too tight for her, the outline of her body clear and full. Pike was weak, dependent on a woman, and how far had he compromised in Ventura?

Carol Pike put on her trench coat. "Let's leave, Carl."

"All right, yes. We'll go home and talk," he said, nodded.

"Of course we will, dear," she said, took his arm.

He gave the bald man, Andy Skinner, some money, thanked him. Skinner seemed sorry to see him go. We all got back into our coats, the chauffeur opened the door, and we struggled out into the hurricane bent against the wind and driving rain.

The shots echoed faint when we were halfway to the car. Something struck the house behind me, sang past my ear. Pike fell, blood on his face. I went down, crawled to him in the mud. Carol Pike was screaming, her mouth open and soundless in the wind. Weaver still stood, staring toward the dark marsh. The chauffeur came to help me. We got Pike up, all fought our way back inside.

"What happened?" Andy Skinner said, ran to Pike.

Pike stood there pale, holding his shoulder that dripped blood. I ripped off his clothing.

"Someone shot at us," I said. "Both of us. Me and Pike."

His wound was small, a flesh wound on the shoulder, the blood spattering on his face.

"Why?" he said, his blue eyes blank over the ragged beard.

"I don't know. Skinner, you better call the police."

The hotel owner shook his head. "Can't, the lines are out. Probably the storm. The wooden bridge is out, too. I just heard. I guess you're all stuck here until it's over."

Until the hurricane ended.

And somewhere outside there was someone with a gun.

21

How many hours had passed I didn't know, day and night were the same. Weaver and I sat in front of the lounge fire. We wore Skinner's old clothes, listened to the old hotel creak and groan, the rage of the wind outside over the black bay. Carl Pike was in his room, resting. Carol was with him. The silent chauffeur sat in a corner with a drink, enigmatic. I didn't know where the Skinners were.

"Why shoot at Pike?" I said.

"Unless he's lying?" Weaver said. "And there's another blackmailer? It would explain shooting at you, too."

"Or unless he's telling the truth. Walter Berger was blackmailing someone, and for killing James McBride. I'm certain of it. Jake Carter knew, and was killed. What does Pike know?"

Weaver was moody. "Is it possible you have it all wrong? Berger not a blackmailer? Carter attacked for some entirely different reason? Not even connected to McBride or IMR?"

I didn't even want to think about that. The nightmare of all police work—off on a totally false track.

"Does Pike know something that changes it all, points at someone else? A different motive for McBride's death?"

"Do you believe Pike, Dan? The whole thing? A kind of poet with a damned sex problem? That's what it adds up to. Is it a con game? He's got someone out there to shoot you, a trick?"

It was always possible. "If he's telling the truth, what does that leave us with? Who killed McBride, and why? Who's out there shooting?"

Weaver said nothing, watched the fire. Windows rattled.

"Carol?" I said. "She wanted IMR's offer, wanted the pressure on Pike. She knew he couldn't turn it down, or she was sure he couldn't. There's a hired professional around."

"A professional? To shoot you? Shooting Pike an error?"

"Because she pushed McBride off that cliff."

Weaver sat up, scowled. "She's capable of it. The princess, the world owes her special treatment. More than ambition, Dan. Her rights. She feels superior, must be favored, be adored. You know, I haven't tried for her. Because she would want me to exist for her. Pike's right about that, he's just too weak. She wouldn't want me, she'd want my position, and she'd take it for herself. One of the elite, attention only to her."

I nodded. "Who else knows we're here? Ruth Montrose?"

Weaver was silent. I looked at him. He nodded.

"Yes. I called her to say where I'd be. You don't think—?"

"She was in California when McBride died."

"But why, Dan? We needed McBride. She wanted him."

"Nugent?"

"He doesn't know we're here."

"How do he and Ruth Montrose get along? He's ambitious."

"They get along well, but Nugent's my man."

"You're so sure?"

He watched the fire. "No, not absolutely. But Nugent's not a killer. Neither is Ruth Montrose or Carl Pike."

"Anybody's a killer given the moment, the motive, the desperation. A flash of insanity. An intolerable instant."

"And never again? A mistake?"

"No right or wrong, Frank? Just mistakes? No individuals? People are just factors in the big picture. Only groups count?"

He sat back watching me, those long legs stretched out, his lean face and drooping eyelid shadowed in the firelight. He seemed to listen to the storm, one with it, the vast world.

"I'm glad we're on the same side, Dan. You'd be a dangerous adversary," he said, smiled at me. "But I wouldn't be afraid of you. You could be a dangerous opponent, except you made a fatal mistake at the start—you believe in absolute truth. I can see it in everything you say and do. Your shabby clothes, your maverick manner. You reject conventions, creature comforts, success in your contemporary world. You prefer to be *right* rather than powerful, to *know* rather than to act, to understand not manage."

"Is that bad?"

"No, only impotent. You know, but you can't do. Haven't you ever wondered why philosophers never had any visible effect on the world? On how people act? Why no one ever listened?"

"I've wondered," I said.

"They spoke ultimate truths. Truth, but it had no relevance to daily living. Irrelevant, Dan. The only truth that counts is relative, what is true for people here and now. What they want now. You can say it's wrong to serve a corporation above all else, and perhaps it is in the absolute. But for today it's right, the way we live. The way people live now. People live in a world they were born to, Dan, not in a pure world."

"Because something is, doesn't make it right," I said.

"Yes it does, Dan. What we believe is true."

Carl Pike stood in the lounge doorway. "He's right, Fortune. Only a fool tries to swim against the stream."

He came into the lounge, his shirt thick with the bandage, and made a drink. He sat on a stool, listened to the wind.

"Too bad you couldn't act on that," Weaver said. "All you need is a full sex life. You'd move the earth."

"Outstare the lightning? Even Shakespeare said it, all the way back. He knew. I'm not so special. All Cleopatra had to do to make Antony fight to the end was sleep with him."

"That's why he lost and Augustus won," Weaver said.

Pike twirled his glass, set it aside. "She's upstairs, angry. She tried the usual way. I walked out. Maybe I'm learning. It hurt, but I did it. I walked out on the job, and I walked out of the bedroom. Maybe I've got a chance yet."

"No you haven't," Weaver said.

"Bad for IMR if I made it, right?" Pike said. He looked at his full drink, and then pushed it farther away. But he didn't turn his back on it. "I don't want our marriage to be one of those where both end up going their separate ways—outside sex, booze, clubs, reading. I want our marriage to be us together."

"She'll never let you, Pike. Not with her," Weaver said.

Pike nodded, touched his full glass. "If I'd been a playboy, living on Daddy's money with all the time in the world to pay attention to her, I'd have done much better. The harder I wanted to work, the worse it got. Odd."

"But IMR was okay? If you worked there?" I asked. "She wanted you to take the job a lot?"

"A lot. The golden opportunity," Pike said, reached toward the glass. He stopped. "My father died without ever having the luck to grow old. He never reached an age of peace, died still young, wanting and hoping and planning. It makes life short."

Weaver got up, poked the fire, put on a fresh log. "When did you ever do good work, Pike? Really? Why did you really marry a woman like Carol? Do you know?"

"Work?" Pike said. "Yes, I did good work. A long time ago, when the titanium process actually got started. It was my original concept. You didn't know that. Jim McBride developed it, but I conceived the basic key. At a time when my life was a total chaos. Three years with a girl who ran me ragged, no money, on the move, but I did more in those three years than in all the years with Carol. Funny."

"Maybe not," Weaver said, stood with his back to the fire, the flame-light playing satanic over his lean face and drooping eye. "I think you married Carol so you *couldn't* work. An excuse not to have to go on, because inside you had no more to offer, no more insights, and you knew it. Or perhaps because you were afraid to really try. You'd done your apprentice research, and inside you were afraid you had nothing else."

"No!" Pike cried. "That's not true!"

"Isn't it?" Weaver laughed.

The crash was like an echo of his laugh. A smashing of glass as if the storm had blown out both window and storm window. But it wasn't the storm. I saw the rifle muzzle come through the smashed window with a scouring of wind and rain. I pushed Pike, went over the bar, shouting:

"Weaver! Drop!"

The two shots exploded like bombs inside the lounge. The mirror behind the bar smashed. A chair above Carl Pike splintered. I had my old cannon out, raised up over the bar, and got off two shots. The rifle barrel vanished, leaving only the wind and rain blowing silent through the smashed window.

After a long minute, I circled and came up on the broken window from the side. No one was there, the hotel yard was empty, nothing moved in the black day except the reeds and rising water.

Skinner was behind me. "Close the inside shutters."

We all closed the inside shutters, stayed out of the line of fire through the windows. Carol Pike and Mrs. Skinner didn't appear. Upstairs, they seemed to have heard nothing over the storm. Weaver turned to all of us:

"We've got to get help. Get the police out here."

"No way," Skinner said. "Who else has a gun? Carl?"

Pike shook his head. Weaver swore:

"Damn it, man, he could attack again anytime!"

"The shutters are up, the doors are locked and solid," Skinner said. "I don't know what's going on, but no one's going out of here until the hurricane's over. The one-armed guy's got a gun, that attacker knows it. He won't try to bust in."

"Why can't we try to get the police?" Pike asked.

"It's a quarter of a mile through the marsh, by now the water's up chest-deep. With the bridge out, you'd have to swim a hundred yards of hurricane water. You're a good swimmer, Carl, but not that good. Then it's five miles to a phone if one's still operating, and creeks in between."

"I'm willing to try," Weaver said.

"No way," Skinner said again. "You'll all just have to bed down here 'til morning. Should blow itself out by then."

Back in the lounge, Pike got a blanket and nailed it up over the shutter on the broken window. It looked like a long night, so we decided to keep watch in pairs. Weaver and Skinner volunteered to watch first. I followed Pike up to our rooms. He didn't even look at his whisky as he left the lounge.

I forced myself to sleep. I was going to need it.

About six, Skinner's wife served dinner. Carol Pike didn't come down. We had fish, beets and French fries—hot and good.

By nine the storm blew even harder, and Pike and I took the watch. I sat at the bar. Pike sat at a table. His drink was untouched on the bar, flat and melted.

"Who's out there?" he said. "Why?"

"I don't know," I said, "do you? He shot at you too."

"He couldn't have. No reason."

"If you didn't kill McBride, maybe you know something that points to who did."

"I never even went to Santa Barbara. They had Jim, only IMR wanted me." He closed his eyes, leaned his head back. "Why kill me? I died when I took IMR's offer. The end of everything I wanted. When there's nothing left to dream, you're dead. A blue death, oxygen-starved. My life is over. The rest is fear, age, diminished powers, nothing."

"Does it have to be, Pike?"

"Maybe it's not so bad," he said. "Once you admit it's all over, maybe you can have peace. Do what you enjoy, even if it's only a poker game. Give them their work, live outside it."

"You believe that?"

"No, it's claptrap, isn't it? What drove you is still there, you can't hide. What stopped you is still there, too. The need and the flaw. But maybe it can be lived with. Maybe I can make it alone. Two weeks now. Maybe I can try, really try. Face up to being alone, even to hurting Carol and the kids if they won't try with me. Damn it, maybe I can!"

Weaver came into the lounge. "Slept enough. Carol won't come down." He looked at Pike. "She seems to be hiding."

"I'll see," Pike said.

He went upstairs, and Weaver and I went around checking the locks and bolts. There was no way of knowing if whoever had shot was still out there or not. The storm covered everything. When we got back to the lounge, Pike still wasn't there. Weaver made himself a drink, wondered about Carol Pike.

"She's not the kind to stay hidden," he said.

"Maybe she and Pike had an—" I began.

We both heard the noise! Somewhere in the rear. A metallic sound, like a rifle barrel hitting against something, a door opening and closing. I got out my cannon, Weaver and I went warily back toward the rear. Weaver saw it first:

"The back door!"

It was closed and locked—but the inside bolt was open! Someone had gone out! We hurried upstairs, called everyone down to the lounge. Carol Pike came last, wrapped in an old robe of Mrs. Skinner's. Pike wasn't there.

"Then it was all a lie!" Weaver said. "He did it all."

"The damn fool's probably gone to try for help!" Skinner said.

"Carol," I said, "Do you know where he's gone? Or why?"

She looked at all of us. "No, I don't know."

Weaver and I took up our watch, the others went back to their rooms. Weaver sipped his drink, his drooping eyelid closed.

"If he's guilty after all, he won't get far," Weaver said.

"If he went for help," I said, "he may not get far either."

After a time we both dozed, and by one A.M. I sensed the storm abating. At three the silence woke me. A strange hush like a vacuum. I woke Weaver. The rain had stopped, the wind was gone. Weaver went to alert Carol Pike and the chauffeur. I went cautiously outside, my gun in hand. Then I heard the sirens. They were across the inlet, and coming toward us. Pike had done it!

I slipped my pistol into my pocket and hurried along the road toward where the wooden bridge had been. The marsh road was still ankle-deep in water. I sloshed ahead—and stopped.

A man lay in the road. A woman in a long raincoat and boots bent over him. The man was Carl Pike. The woman had a gun in her hand pointed at my chest. We were hidden from house and inlet.

"How's real estate in New Jersey?" I said.

She was the big, mannish blonde. As professional as ever. The pistol was steady, the safety off. I made no sudden moves. Carl Pike lay on his back, blood around a hole in his head, a gun on the ground near him.

"Didn't Pike pay you?" I said.

She looked all around. "Dead an hour or two, I'd say. One shot from that thirty-two. Looks like suicide."

"The police'll want to know your client's name," I said.

She said nothing. Two mercenaries from opposite sides.

"Look," I said, "do you know what you're mixed up in? A man named McBride was killed in Santa Barbara. Maybe Pike there did it, maybe not. If not, someone else did, and was being blackmailed. The blackmailer's dead too—both of them. That's three murders, maybe four now. Tell me who hired you."

She watched me carefully, considering my face and arm.

"The police'll get it out of you," I said.

"The police are on the other side of the inlet," she said, and began to back away. The gun still steady on me, she vanished into the tall bulrushes.

I heard her for a time, and then silence. I bent down over Carl Pike. He was dead. Maybe two hours. The gun was near his right hand, the caliber looked right. Probably his gun, it had his initials on the butt: CP. There were some small footprints, maybe the blonde's, all indistinct in mud. His clothes were sodden, and he wore no shoes, as if he'd swum the inlet on his way back to the hotel. Nothing else except the contents of his wallet strewn around where it had fallen out. I looked them over: credit cards, pictures of his children, some money, a bill from a Ventura liquor store, a Blue Cross card. The usual junk.

"Is he—?" Weaver stood behind me with Carol Pike.

I nodded. Carol turned her face away, leaned against Weaver's chest. He looked at me, shook his head.

22

It was dawn by the time the police got the body and us across the inlet and into Toms River. The old shore town on its winding waterway was a wreck of shattered piers and beached boats, trees down everywhere, houses flooded and empty.

At the headquarters a captain took charge. Carol identified the gun from the road as Pike's, Andy Skinner told about the shooting at the hotel, and I told him about the whole case. I left out the blonde pro. As soon as the Captain heard that Pike had been wanted in a murder investigation, he nodded and closed his mind: Pike's own gun, one shot—suicide. Andy Skinner didn't agree.

"He didn't have a gun, I asked him," Skinner said.

"He probably lied, Andy," the Captain said. "Fortune was after him, maybe he knew his story wouldn't hold up, planned an escape. Then," a shrug, "knew he'd never make it."

"Someone tried to kill him out there!" Skinner insisted.

"We'll investigate, but that was a rifle, maybe only aimed at Fortune. Pike was shot with a small pistol, his own."

IMR had a car down for Weaver by seven A.M. The police let him, Carol Pike and the chauffeur go after getting statements. I decided to wait for the medical and ballistics reports, the results of the search of the marshes out at the hotel. Weaver told me not to worry about fees, IMR would take care of it all.

"I'll only pad it a little," I said.

The reports were in before eight A.M.—one .32-cal. bullet in the head, bruises from his swim for help; his own gun was the one; shell casings found in the marsh, tire tracks from two cars on the mainland side of the inlet, no sign of anyone now.

"That's it, then," the Captain said. "Looks like we've got no case, and you've solved yours."

"Maybe, but someone was out in that marsh shooting."

"A third blackmailer." The Captain was definite. "Trying to cover himself. With Pike dead, he'll fade out."

"Pike went through the marsh in a hurricane, swam that inlet, struggled five miles to a phone to call help," I said. "Then he did it all again to return, didn't even wait to go back with you. He got a hundred yards from the hotel, and then decided to kill himself? Maybe he suddenly cracked, but it's pretty thin."

"Then who do you think shot him? With his own gun."

"The only thing I'm sure of is that Weaver or I didn't."

I got a bus to New York at eight-thirty. There was water and damage all up the coast, people picking through the debris, but this was megalopolis, and traffic was already moving fast and heavy on the Parkway. I closed my eyes. Suicide would answer all the questions, close it. Attractive. IMR would even pay me, and well if I knew Weaver. But a man doesn't perform a feat like Pike's struggle to get help, and then shoot himself a hundred yards from home. Later maybe, not then. Unless, at that exact moment, he heard or saw something that showed him the game was up. Possible, but . . . ?

For murder there were two possible motives. Pike had killed McBride after all, and there was a third blackmailer afraid of both Pike and the police, out to cover himself. Pike hadn't killed anybody, but, in some way, knew who had. Maybe didn't even know he knew, but the real murderer taking no chances. Who? With hired hands in the picture—anyone. Anyone could have hired Jake Carter, Berger and Pike killed. But not Dr. McBride.

Someone who had been out in California that day. Carol Pike because she wanted Pike to have the IMR job? Hiding in her room at

Skinner's Hotel because Pike knew she'd killed McBride? Going out to meet Pike, Weaver and I asleep in the lounge?

Ruth Montrose? She'd been in California, knew we were at Skinner's Hotel. Nugent? Where had he been on August fourteenth? In Europe with Weaver, or in California? He was the only one without a real alibi for the attack on Jake Carter.

But where the hell was their motive? Why kill Carl Pike?

I called Weaver from the West Side Terminal. Neither he nor Emily were at the office. There was no answer at Weaver's apartment. I took a taxi down to Tenth Street. Leslie buzzed back at once, waited in her doorway in a thin robe. She looked like she hadn't slept. She hugged her breasts with folded arms.

"He didn't come. I waited all last night."

I told her where Weaver had been and why. She sat down, limp, relief all over her dark face. She lit a cigarette.

"I guess I'm in love, Dan," she said, shook her head as if it was hard to believe. "He's quite a guy, isn't he?"

"He is," I agreed. "A winner, right?"

"No, not anymore. Not just that. A lot more than that, Dan. I loved Jake, but this is something else." She stared at space, at whatever it was with her and Weaver. "So this Carl Pike killed Jake? Over blackmail?"

"Maybe, and maybe not. Weaver hasn't called this morning?"

"Not yet."

Probably still in Short Hills, doing his duty by Carol Pike. I wondered if Pike was due any pension from IMR after a month? Probably not, but maybe IMR would do something for the widow. My questions about Nugent and Montrose would have to wait. Unless Emily Hahn could answer them, or Leslie.

"Leslie, did Weaver ever talk to you about the case? Did he say anything about Ruth Montrose or Nugent?"

"Only that Montrose had been his mistress once, and that she was an ambitious woman, competitive. He laughed about it, called it healthy, always outdoing each other to improve IMR. He said she kept him on his toes."

"Anything about her and McBride?"

She nodded. "When he was angry once over Carl Pike giving IMR trouble, he said Ruth Montrose had blown the deal."

"Blown? But McBride was dead."

"I think Frank meant something before he died."

It slid into place like an oiled key. Weaver had said it himself—*"McBride chose to work elsewhere."* Ruth Montrose had probably told him a month ago that McBride had rejected IMR's offer—*before* McBride died. Then, after McBride was dead, had to make Weaver think he'd misunderstood. I heard Carl Pike's voice—*"They had Jim . . ."* Titanium Development *had* McBride. Ambiguous, but there. What Pike had known that was dangerous—that Jim McBride was going to accept Titanium Development's job. It took away Pike and Carol's motive, and gave a new motive. But I had to be sure.

"I'm using your phone," I said to Leslie.

I got a seat on an eleven A.M. flight to Los Angeles, a connection to Santa Barbara.

"Tell Weaver I'll see him late tonight or tomorrow."

I went down and got a cab, rode up to tell Emily where I was going. I used my key—it makes a man feel good to have a key to his woman's apartment, a sign that she wants him. She wasn't there. I looked around for paper to leave a note—and I froze. Her closet was open, a green slack suit hung there.

I sat down. Old Ben Maddox—*"Big woman in green pants . . . didn't see her hair . . . Tall woman, big all over."* The big blonde professional wasn't the only "big" woman. A third blackmailer? Emily had been close to Walter Berger, had talked often to Jake Carter while he chased after his lease, had talked with Carl Pike. Where had she been on August fourteenth?

I felt cold, a lump in my belly. Who else had known I was going after Carl Pike at the Jersey Shore? Emily had because I'd told her.

Not where, I hadn't known then, but with my wait for the Mercedes it would have been a simple matter to follow me to Short Hills and then down to the shore hotel. But not alone, no. With Ruth Montrose? Or the blonde professional? Or Tom Nugent?

I left my note for her, but my hand wasn't steady.

23

I landed in Santa Barbara at three P.M., rented a car, drove out to Titanium Development on its cliffs above the blue, rolling sea. I thought of Carl Pike and the peace he'd wanted, the quality of life he'd found and wanted out here. I wondered if he would have made his break. Probably not, few men can escape themselves, but maybe he would have, the feat to get help through the hurricane a symbol. I wanted to think so.

At Titanium Development, Dr. Sturgis still wore the same stained laboratory coat, nodded me to a seat. I told him about Carl Pike. He looked stunned.

"Both of them then? Damn, what a waste to science!"

"You said McBride called IMR from your house. Was it a long call?"

"No, very brief."

"What gave you the feeling he liked the job here?"

"Well, his eagerness mostly. The way he talked about our smallness, the chance to do his work unhindered and *finish* it," Sturgis said, thought. "His emphasis on the length of his contract. He seemed to want to be sure of time and a relatively free hand. In fact, I had the impression he'd made up his mind he liked our offer before he came up if the terms were right."

"He could have told IMR he was leaning to you before he came," I said. "Warned them. He did call them before he came, his wife said so. Then up here just a brief call to reject them."

"I can't really say for sure, Mr. Fortune."

I thanked him, drove south on 101 in the brilliant late September sun and blue sky, the sea and the islands clear off to the right. I wasn't thinking of the scenery, I was thinking of the anger of IMR when James McBride decided to go to another company. Enough for murder. No, not in itself, and maybe not for most people, but for a tough, competitive, ambitious executive devoted to IMR, out to go far, prove her importance?

Or someone devoted to a boss? Even in love with her boss, furious at a man who was injuring her boss? Lashing out? A giant devoted to his leader?

By then I was in Ventura and parking at Foley Institute. It still bustled with activity, hummed with air-conditioning, oblivious to the sky and mountains around it. Dr. Foley was as gracious as ever, offered his Loewenbrau, beaming at me like some Madison Avenue buddha. I told him about Pike, and he stopped beaming. He looked wary.

"Mrs. McBride says McBride was disturbed then, Foley, even angry. What would make him angry about good job offers?"

"I have no idea."

"It sounds like there was something he didn't like."

"Really?"

"Maybe he didn't like IMR, didn't want to work for them."

Foley tented his hands, chewed a fingernail.

"Would IMR have been annoyed if he turned them down?"

"I doubt they'd have been pleased," Foley said.

"Angry? Furious? Maybe cheated?"

He leaned forward, half up. "I'm sorry, but I must—"

"You gave me the idea McBride was leaving you for a better job, you couldn't keep him against such a good offer. But Mrs. McBride says you'd told him you couldn't renew his contract. In short, you were firing McBride. Pike too, later."

"We do have budget problems. It so happens—"

"It happened to be McBride who had to be cut?" I said. "He wasn't being hired away, Foley, you were making him go. You were selling him to IMR. They paid you to force him to take their job. But Titanium Development loused it up. IMR was cheated."

"I don't have to discuss my business with you!"

I sat back. "You run a kind of slave market, don't you, Foley? You grab talent, then sell it to big corporations. A scientific minor league. But McBride balked, he didn't like IMR's ways. I'll bet Ruth Montrose was flaming mad."

"All right," Foley said, folded his arms, his bald head shining with sweat. "There's nothing at all wrong with it. I find good men, let them develop until the big companies want them. It's a good service. We have to live, too."

"Nothing wrong—except you don't tell the scientists. You don't tell them you sell them, and you don't share the loot."

"It's perfectly legal!"

"Did you sell Pike, too? Cut-rate as a substitute, or maybe double rate because he was the only one left for that process?"

"I received a small bonus, yes."

"IMR got screwed all ways. Two payments, no scientists."

"I have no blame for Pike! He was at IMR."

"One healthy scientist, good teeth, strong back," I said, disgusted. "Had McBride turned IMR down?"

Foley was sullen. "I told you I don't—"

"Quadruple murder," I said. "I can get the police."

He squirmed. "I'm not sure if McBride had decided, but I think so. I got a call from Ruth Montrose a few days earlier. McBride had warned IMR he was seriously considering Titanium Development. The fool! IMR was too big, too ruthless, too anonymous! He'd be regimented. All that money. The idiot!"

I had two more questions, one I didn't want to ask.

"Was Weaver's assistant Tom Nugent out here then?"

"Not that I know."

"Weaver's secretary, Emily Hahn?"

"I couldn't say, I never met her."

I got up. At the door, I turned back. "Pike knew that Jim McBride was against IMR, didn't he?"

"Probably."

"Carol Pike?"

"I'm not sure. McBride didn't like her very much."

I went out.

It was almost six P.M. now. I was hungry. I went to the Pierpont Inn and this time got some dinner. I was pretty sure now what had happened, only a few details were missing. It didn't seem like a one-man, or one-woman, job, and I had no real proof that McBride had turned IMR down. I finished my dinner and drove out to Carl Pike's old beach cottage at the foot of the barranca off 101.

The cottage was still unoccupied, the old furniture still there. A whisky bottle and two dirty glasses stood in the kitchen, but the drinks had evaporated, the glasses used almost a week ago. I went into the garage laboratory and searched for any note that might show Carl Pike had known McBride's decision. I didn't find anything. Just uncompleted research notes. Carl Pike's dream that would never be finished now.

It was too late now to get back to New York before the early morning hours, and I was tired. I wanted some drinks and a swim. I wanted to think about Emily Hahn. Maybe I didn't want to go back to New York. Did I really think Emily could be involved? No, I didn't. But there was a faint doubt. A doubt I knew I would never have had about Marty. I had to do a lot of thinking about Emily Hahn.

I checked into a beach motel, borrowed a bathing suit, and swam a long way out into the blue, rolling ocean.

It was growing dark on the Upper East Side when the taxi from Kennedy dropped me in front of Emily Hahn's apartment, and I went up. I used my key. She was there, wearing that navy blue dress with the white collar I'd first seen her in. She saw my face.

"Dan? What's wrong? What happened in California?"

I told her.

"You mean . . . Someone pushed McBride off that cliff because he turned down the job with IMR? No, Dan!"

"Anger. Not intentional. But Berger saw it, blackmailed, there had to be a cover-up."

"There must be another reason, Dan," she said.

"There still could be. But IMR is in the middle."

"All those murders? Someone at IMR?"

"Loyal to the company, or to someone in the company," I said. "Emily, where were you the night Jake and Berger died?"

"Me? Dan—?" She got a cigarette, but didn't light it. She stood looking away. "I was here, at home. After I left you at the athletic club, I came home. Alone."

"Ben Maddox said he saw a woman. A big woman, tall, in a green pants suit."

"Not me! What else did he see? Did he see me attack?"

"He didn't see the attack itself. Just saw Jake run out of the office with a wrench in his—"

I heard old Ben Maddox again—"*Carter come runnin' from the shack with somethin' in his hand, and . . .*" The wrench! Jake had had it. Not the man who attacked him, but *Jake*. All at once I knew who had hit Jake Carter, and why, and there could only be one motive for the whole thing.

"We'll talk," I said to Emily. "Later."

"Yes," she said.

The doctor who'd operated on Jake was on duty at Roosevelt Hospital. He was sad about Jake, he'd really hoped to save him. The operation had gone so well.

"He hit that transmission too hard. Too much damage."

"You said a wrench broke his cheekbone, knocked him down."

"No. I said a wrench could have done it, since the police found one. Many things could have done it. A steel bar, a club. But something swung hard enough to knock him down violently."

"A fist?"

"Well, yes. But it would have to have been a strong man. To make him fall with such force. A very strong man."

My sportswriter contact was having dinner at Downey's. I showed him the oval topaz-colored stone with the line of small diamonds in the center I'd found near Jake Carter. He agreed it looked like a miniature football.

"I'll call around, Dan."

I put a beer on his bill, waited. It took about fifteen minutes. He came back pleased with himself.

"I'll check more, but everyone's pretty sure it's from a ring given out about ten years ago by a Booster Club when the Montana Tech team went to the Oil Bowl."

"Tom Nugent was at Montana Tech?"

"Best tackle they ever had."

The doorman at Weaver's Park Avenue building was nervous. He hadn't wanted to hold me for the police that night.

"Mr. Weaver told me, you know? He's a big tenant."

"He called down himself to tell you?"

"No, Mr. Nugent called for him."

I went back downtown to my office. It would waste half an hour, but I wanted my gun with me.

24

The building was an old one on Riverside Drive. There was no door-man, and no elevator operator. The apartment was on the fourth floor. I heard voices inside, listened. They were speaking in Spanish. One smooth and quick, the other thick and stumbling. I got out my gun, rang.

The voices stopped. There was a moment of silence, then Tom Nugent opened the door. Massive, he filled the doorway, his head touching the top frame. He looked at the gun in my hand, he looked at me. He didn't seem very surprised.

"Go in, Tom," I said. "Stay five feet away from me."

He backed inside almost soundless, amazingly light on his feet. He stopped in the center of his living room. A small room, and a small apartment. He didn't spend much on rent, or on furniture. The small room was clean, neat and sparse. There were shelves full of books on business, charts on the walls, a desk of notes and textbooks. I saw his visitor—a record player on a table, he was learning Spanish. The room of a man trying hard to get ahead. Ambitious, hard-working, sober.

"You should have stayed with the books," I said.

"What do you want, Fortune?"

He knew. He hadn't even asked why I had the gun.

"It wasn't for money, was it?" I said. "Loyalty, IMR forever. You killed Jake Carter, I found your ring-stone. He tried to fight you, used a wrench, and you hit him harder than you'd intended. Then you came home, but went out again later that night after Walter Berger. Easy to slip out of this building. You drove Berger's body to Short Hills, took the train back from Newark. It was you out in that marsh in the hurricane. You and that blonde professional, but you had the rifle. An ambush for me, and for Pike if necessary."

Nugent licked his mustache.

"But not for money, and not for yourself," I said. "You didn't kill James McBride, and probably not Berger. McBride turned down IMR, was knocked over that cliff in a flash of anger. A mistake. So Pike had to be hired, but that wasn't the worst. Walter Berger was out there in Santa Barbara and saw McBride go over the cliff. He had a young and very greedy wife. Her idea, the blackmail, I'd guess, but Berger handled it. That's why he forgot the lease renewal, why he was out of the office. Busy and scared. Afraid his victim would try to get rid of him. He had reason to be scared, I would have been. Poison. That's not your weapon."

He still said nothing.

"Don't be too loyal to IMR," I said. "That's why you did it, wasn't it, Tom? That's why you killed Jake Carter. The way Jake died, and why, finally told me who did it."

I saw the alarm in his eyes, the tension.

"The key was Jake's connection to all of it, to Berger and Pike," I said. "The answer was—*he didn't have any connection*. No real connection to Berger, or Pike, or any of it. None at all. He wasn't part of any blackmail, he knew nothing. You hit Jake for the same reason you called the police on me that same night, but you hit Jake too hard because he fought back with that wrench. An accident, and just because you were loyal, and wanted—"

I saw the curtain suddenly blow in at his open window, and felt the air move against my neck. I half turned. A reflex, but it was enough. Before I could correct myself, turn back, Nugent had me. With one hand he lifted me off the floor by my throat, with the other he swept my gun away. I kicked, choked.

Frank Weaver came into the room, bent and picked up my gun.

"Let him down, Nugent," he said.

Nugent put me down. He stayed near me. The outside door was open. Weaver had keys to a lot of places. He closed the outside door, put my gun into his pocket, his drooping eyelid twitching as if he hated guns.

"So you know Nugent killed Carter and why, Dan?" he said.

I nodded, my throat sore from Nugent's brief grip. "In your apartment that night, you said, *'Can't anyone stop you people from badgering me?'* An offhand remark, you were exasperated and tired out from chasing after Carl Pike. But Nugent took you literally. He called the police to cool me off, keep me away from you, and he went down to the parking lot to lean on Jake to get him to stop bothering you about the lease. But Jake grabbed a wrench to fight back, and Nugent hit too hard. A favor for his boss."

"All Nugent wanted to do," Weaver said, weary, "was to stop Carter from badgering me. Carter had no connection to the rest of it. Nugent thought he was helping, an overeager idiot!" He shook his head, mystified. "The whole mess because of fools and losers. One man too stupid to accept a good job, another a damned pure poet! A parking-lot owner, and a one-armed detective. An old plodding exec, and his greedy wife. The lame, the halt, and the blind!"

I let him talk, my mind busy with escape. Somehow, I knew I had to escape or this was going to be the end for me. Nugent would do whatever Weaver told him. Weaver wouldn't have a gun, that wasn't his style, and mine was on safety in his pocket. There was only Nugent. Nugent was enough.

"But," Weaver said, "one of that whole troop of nobodies had to be smart, very smart. I'm truly sorry about Carter, Dan, but the worst part of Nugent's overzealousness was that it brought you into the affair too deeply."

"And Walter Berger knew he'd hit Jake, too," I said. "Berger was keeping an eye on you and Nugent, scared of you. So he saw Nugent at the parking lot, upped his blackmail on you."

"Poor Walter," Weaver said sadly.

"How did you get to California on the fourteenth?" I asked him, to keep him talking. "Over the Pole?"

He nodded. "McBride called Berger on the thirteenth, said he was just about ready to sign with Titanium Development. We'd already paid Foley twenty thousand dollars to make sure we got McBride and his process! McBride had warned us earlier that he might turn us down. I'd left word that I be contacted at once. Berger called me in London. I told Berger to meet me in Santa Barbara, and flew over the Pole. When we arrived at Titanium Development, I didn't want to be seen, waited outside to try to get McBride alone, talk to him. When I saw him come out and walk out along the cliff path, I followed him."

His lean face set in deep, tense lines as if remembering that cliff path. "I caught up with him at that narrow spot, demanded an explanation. He said IMR was too big, too powerful, too ruthless and indifferent to real science. All IMR wanted was profit! He practically told me to go to hell! I was furious. We'd made a fair, even generous offer. We'd paid Foley. We needed that process, and no one else was going to have it! We deserved it, we had to have it. It was our right. One man wasn't—!" He took a slow, deep breath. His eyelid jumped. "So I hit him. More than once. He . . . he went over the edge. I found a way down to where he fell, but he was dead. I didn't know if I'd been seen, there were houses. I slipped back to our car, flew back to London. Later I called Ruth Montrose, told her to hire Pike. We had to have the process."

"In a way that was too bad," I said. Nugent never took his eyes off me. "Pike was as much trouble as McBride. And Berger—after his wife put him up to it. You paid him at first, right? Did he want a promotion, too? I suppose so, wife's a snob."

"Not to protect myself, Dan. You understand? For IMR. If it were only myself, I'd have gone to the police at once. But I couldn't have the scandal for IMR, the public investigation. Then, I'm vital to IMR just now. Not as a person, as a function. I do the best job on my level we can get at the moment. I had to protect IMR. You do understand, Dan?"

I understood. Maybe not exactly what he wanted me to, but I understood. He stretched his arms wide, a hopeless gesture.

"But Berger saw Nugent at that parking lot, found Carter, and called me. It was escalating. Carter's death would be investigated. You were involved. If anyone reached Walter Berger . . . ? I told him to come to my apartment."

"Cyanide," I said. I began to feel desperate. How long could I keep him talking? When he stopped—? "Something you had around from one of your ore plants. After Nugent took his body to Short Hills, you made up your story about calling him over the lease to hide that he'd been watching you, hoped we'd think he killed Jake Carter over some shakedown."

"I kept trying to have you stopped, Dan. I knew that if I was ever placed in Santa Barbara, or my motive guessed, someone out there might identify me, my flight could be traced. I'd lost a key somewhere too. To my tennis locker. I didn't know if it had been found."

"It had been," I said. "When Pike called Carol, she talked to you first, right? You had her invite me along. An ambush. For me, and for Pike if necessary. You were afraid he could give your motive, but you didn't want to lose him for IMR if you could help it. But you had to give him up, signal Nugent to shoot him. The trouble was, Pike being shot at made me figure there had to be some other motive. Then I realized why Jake Carter had been attacked, and you had to be the killer."

"How did you realize what Nugent had done?"

"There's an old man who hated Jake Carter so much he was watching the parking lot all that night. He saw Jake run out with a wrench. *Jake* had the wrench. Jake was hit, his cheek fractured, by a fist. Who could hit that hard?"

He nodded, almost pleased. "I said you were dangerous, didn't I?"

"No, you said I would have been except for my hang-up on absolute truth. You said that gives you the edge."

"It does, doesn't it? I'm sorry, Dan, I'm not a murderer. I simply can't let IMR be hurt over one small mistake. I had to stop Berger, and I have to stop you."

"For IMR," I said. Nugent hadn't relaxed a hair. If—?

"IMR is my only reason for existing. I'm not important except as a part of IMR."

"What does IMR exist for, Weaver?"

"For everyone, Dan. The country. The world. It makes life good for everyone."

"No," I said. "It exists for itself. No country, no world. It hasn't got the same goals or rules. Jake Carter was people. He lived in a world that's supposed to be, but isn't. IMR is in a world that is, a world IMR made for itself. It rules. A minority that runs things for itself, controls the majority."

"A minority always rules, Dan. Everywhere. Societies have to be controlled, and the majority can't do that."

"But we keep on trying," I said, and it had a sound of finality, the wrap-up. I had to go on, keep it going. "There I go again, right? The absolutist. The perfect world where the majority, all of us, run ourselves, are free to—"

"I'm sorry, Dan," Weaver said. "Nugent, bring him—"

The big blonde came out of the bedroom. The old building had a fire escape. She had a gun. It aimed at Weaver.

25

"His pocket," I croaked. "My gun."

She got my gun, watched both Weaver and Nugent. She wore a green pants suit.

"Aviva Galt," she said. "Licensed in Philadelphia. Weaver hired me to find Carl Pike that first day. I almost caught up with Pike at the parking lot that night, but missed him. Then Weaver told me to find out what you knew, and to discourage you. I don't mind tailing, bugging, searching, a little beating-up or slowing a snooper down, or even throwing a scare with a rifle from a marsh. But I'm not paid for murder."

"Miss Galt," Weaver said, "I'll pay you a lot more—"

Nugent, loyal to the end, tried. She shot him down. A pro, she took no chances. She shot three times, and Nugent fell between her and Weaver. He lay there, breathing hard. Weaver's eyelid jerked as if in pain. His eyes were sick and wet, he brushed at them. Then he looked at Aviva Galt.

"I didn't count on this," he said.

I called Gazzo and an ambulance.

It took some sorting out. The ambulance took Nugent, and Weaver knew his rights. He called his lawyers, insisted on waiting for them. Gazzo didn't push him, the Captain knew the power of IMR. Instead, Gazzo got on the telephone and started to round everyone up for statements later downtown. He was aware of the caliber of the lawyers Weaver would whistle up. Even if Nugent lived, nothing said he'd talk, and Walter Berger was the only first-degree murder.

Weaver sat quietly. He knew how to wait. Aviva Galt leaned in a corner watching, she wasn't a talker. I sat still shaking inside. I didn't hide from what could have happened, Weaver did what he had to. He shook his head at me, approving:

"So you beat me, Dan."

"Maybe relative doesn't have the edge."

"No," he said. "Every now and then one of the enemy proves stronger than he should be. It doesn't really change anything, just a small dislocation. A casualty or two. Call me a casualty. IMR goes on."

"So do we," I said. "You'll probably even get off, maybe a slap on the wrist. You'll have good lawyers. That's the way it is. I don't stop trying. Freedom means risk, Pike said it."

"I'll fight, but it's not important," Weaver said. "What happens to me isn't relevant. I failed my duty. I may not go to prison, but I'll lose what counts to me."

When his lawyers finally arrived, somewhere near dawn, they didn't come alone. Three of them, and Ruth Montrose was with them. The lawyers went into immediate debate with Gazzo and an assistant district attorney he'd called fast. Ruth Montrose sat facing Weaver smoking one of her long cigarettes.

"The Board met," she said. "Your defense was voted, and we're issuing a statement that you acted on your own without IMR's knowledge. You'll make the same statement, right?"

Weaver nodded.

"Sam Ross is making a personal statement deploring your actions, but accepting moral responsibility for the mistake of hiring and promoting you. He offered his resignation, the Board officially rejected it, asked him to continue in office. You were discharged, of course. I've been elected the new executive vice president effective immediately."

"Good," Weaver said. "We'll discuss the delicate matters later when I've a better picture of the immediate future."

"Fine," Ruth Montrose said, stood. "I'll ask Hahn to help me with the routine details. Your wife has been told, she'll be to see you as soon as the lawyers think it politic. We'll pay for your defense, naturally, but we won't be meeting again until it's settled. I think that covers it, Frank."

"You'll do a fine job, Ruth."

She nodded. "It could easily have been me who met McBride."

"My responsibility, my mistake," Weaver said. "Good-bye, Ruth, do a job, eh?"

She left. I studied Weaver's face. It was lean and calm.

"IMR goes on," I said. "Yet IMR was the real killer."

"There you go, Dan," Weaver smiled. "Absolute. I made a mistake, not IMR."

"Tell me," I said, "is there a Sam Ross? I've never seen him. President and chairman. Or is there just IMR itself, a graven image to serve?"

"The Bible now, Dan? We don't live in a commune or a wilderness. We live with color TV, freezers and highways, and IMR gives them to us."

"Thanks," I said.

"It's amazing, but the trouble with Carl Pike really did me in, you know? Without that I'd never have been so harried, Nugent would never have killed Carter, you'd never have gone on. In this day and age, destroyed by a sex problem. Amazing."

"Amazing a man has a sex problem in this day and age."

He laughed, "Yes. The lame, halt and blind, Dan."

"They aren't what brought you down," I said.

"Then don't tell me what did, Dan," he said. "I probably wouldn't understand what you were talking about anyway."

"No," I said, "I don't think you would."

Downtown everyone was there to give their statements. A parade from Carol Pike and Marie Berger, through Owen Pakula and an assistant district attorney flown in fast from Santa Barbara, to Aviva Galt and Andy Skinner. Marie Berger acted as if she'd never seen me before. She buttonholed Weaver's lawyers about Walter Berger's pension. She'd do fine.

Leonore Weaver arrived composed and well-bred for the cameras. She had a distinguished-looking man with her. Her father. They were both firm, it was all some mistake, Frank Weaver would be vindicated. All some kind of political plot.

Leslie and Emily Hahn came out. Emily looked away from me. Leslie looked beaten, her dark eyes almost haunted.

"I doubted Jake, didn't I?" she said. "I wasn't sure he was honest. I'll have to pay for that, Dan. An honest, hard-working man trying to live the way he'd been told he should. He believed it—be independent, work hard. He didn't know the cards were all stacked against him in favor of the IMRs. He had to claw and scrape, while IMR took good care of itself."

She was beating herself. And not just over Jake.

"I don't blame Frank, not for what we did. I have to have a man, so I grabbed the best, fell in love. I guess I never really left that belly-dance club, still living only through men. Jake, too. Making him work so hard for *me* he got killed! So desperate to succeed he badgered Weaver too much!"

"No one's fault, Leslie," I said. "Just—"

"An accident? Jake died for no reason at all? Because Frank Weaver was worried over killing McBride, and Tom Nugent wanted to please the boss? Okay, but what made Jake so desperate? What made Nugent need to please his boss so much?"

I had no answer. She did.

"I'm going to try to find out why Jake had to be so desperate, why Nugent had to serve IMR so hard. What makes us tick, Dan? I'm going to see if I can find how to live without a man. Me and Emily, we've got a lot in common we find. We both made the same mistakes, believed the same things."

I looked at Emily Hahn. "I'm sorry. I doubted, too."

"You had a reason," Emily said.

"Not really," I said. "A mistake of mine. The woman at the lot that night had to have been Aviva Galt, and she was. Looking for Carl Pike. But I didn't have enough certainty, did I?"

"That takes time, Dan," Emily said.

"Yeh," I agreed. "So, no more men?"

"Not for a while. No more playing the office wife," she said. "It's not you, though, Dan. It's me. It's time I found something to do for myself. Something worth doing by itself."

I nodded. They went out together. Now I didn't have any woman. Not even a comfortable memory of Marty. Alone, with my building coming down. Poor me.

I watched Carol Pike come out and ask a cop where she could get a cup of coffee. He directed her to a diner up the block. She was wearing her most "chaste" blue dress, and she looked very good. I was still looking after her when Aviva Galt came up beside me.

"You were lucky," she said.

"Weaver was unlucky," I said. "Berger neglected his work because of his blackmail, Leslie brought me in to help."

"In our trade we need some luck. How about a drink?"

"Make it coffee," I said.

We went out into the Lower Manhattan morning, and up to the diner where Carol Pike sat alone at a table. We joined her. Her eyes were wet and haggard.

"Did he have to kill Carl?" she said. "What am I going to do, Dan?"

"He didn't kill Carl. You did."

She spilled her coffee, "Are you out of—!"

"You shot Carl," I said.

She wiped angrily at her blue dress. Aviva Galt watched.

"That's nasty, Dan," Carol Pike said.

"He had no reason to kill himself. Weaver was with me. Nugent was in the marsh with Aviva there, and he'd have used his rifle. Carl wasn't carrying that gun. You were. There were no men's tracks, only women's. That bill from the Ventura liquor store was dated when you met me out there. After we talked that evening, you bought a bottle, went back to the cottage. The bottle's out there. Carl never went back there. The bill fell from your purse, not his wallet. When you took out the gun."

She wet her soft lips. "Dan, you can't believe—?"

In the diner people were looking at us. I took her arm, raised her from the chair, and walked her out. I walked her back toward police headquarters.

"He was going to quit IMR, wasn't he?" I said, walking her beside me toward the police building. "He was really going to quit IMR this time. Live his way, or try to. He wanted you to try with him, talked about it to you. But he was going to make his break with or without you, and you knew it. That's why you were hiding in your room down there."

She tried to pull away, drag back. Her blue eyes were fixed on the entrance to the police building ahead. "Dan, no! Carl would never—"

"He was going to ruin all your plans, hopes. Everything you wanted, had pushed him so hard to get for you. When he went out into that storm, you knew he'd really leave you if he had to."

"Dan, please, you're wrong! You—!"

"A crazy moment," I said. "Anger and hate. Weaver said it, the world owes you special treatment. More than ambition. What you want is your right to have, you must have it, and men exist for you. When you realized that Carl was really going to break, would leave you, could go on without you, it flipped you out."

We were at the entrance now. She stopped. She looked at the wide doorway, at the police going in and out. She spoke low.

"I knew," she said. "He told me, and when he went out in that hurricane, I knew. I watched for him. When I saw him coming back, I went out. Oh, he was so proud of himself! He said he was going to do it. We'd live his way, or he'd live alone. I tried to . . . to . . . but he pushed me away! He pushed me! Rejected *me!* Ruining everything . . . I shot! I . . . shot him!"

"Yeh," I said. "You shot him."

She was crying. "I didn't mean to . . . I . . . A mistake, Dan. Crazy out in that storm. I . . . I'm so alone. I need a man. Dan, please? I want a man, Dan. You and I—"

I watched her face, that slim, full body.

"I can't prove it," I said. "I won't try. Go home."

She blinked. "But . . . ? I thought—"

"Go home. Go on. Go home now."

She walked away along the crowded street. Slowly at first, looking back. Not sure, not trusting me. That was good, she'd worry for a time. She began to walk faster, stopped looking back, and vanished among the hurrying people. She'd worry, and then she'd find an explanation to live with. She'd justify it, and forget. Probably find another man. Richer.

I started back to the diner. Maybe I could prove enough, and maybe I couldn't, but she wouldn't kill again. A moment of rage, hate and fear, and Carl Pike would have wanted it this way. Their trouble had been no one's fault, and there were the children. Children need someone. They were part of her, of all she wanted. For them, she'd be a good enough mother. They'd grow.

I sat down with Aviva Galt, sipped my coffee.

"You could have had her, you know," Aviva said.

"Maybe," I agreed, "maybe not. She's not good at loving."

So I had no woman. Free even of memory, and alone. Carl Pike had said it—you can't have both freedom and security, and I'm not secure all alone. No more than Pike had been.

"How about that drink?" I said. "My apartment, maybe?"

Aviva smiled. "You think we could get to like each other?"

"We could try," I said.

She got up. A big woman, mannish, but curved female. I followed her out. It's warmer in security. That's why most of us are never free.

THE END

A Sneak Peek at the next Dan Fortune Mystery

**Read the first chapter
of the next exciting Dan Fortune mystery**

***The Blood-Red Dream*
by Dennis Lynds
#8 in the Edgar Award-winning Dan Fortune mystery series**

It was an April night, raining outside. Inside the church, the pew's seat was hard, and the occasional shuffle of my wet feet was the only sound in the rows of empty pews under the high shadows of the narrow, vaulted ceiling.

I waited.

The church, on First Avenue near the river, was dim, and echoing, and filled with the odor of burning votive candles and old stone. St. Stanislaus Roman Catholic, services four days a week in Hungarian, three days in Serbo-Croatian, Faded tapestries hung from the side arches, and the altar and cross were old and darkened by time and the grime of New York.

There was a sense of the ancient and the far-away here, an echo of the Dark Ages. It seemed more alien even than the Polish Roman Catholic churches I'd known as a boy before my old man changed our name to Fortune. Somewhere behind the altar a radio played faintly. Maybe I dozed, I suppose I did.

When I opened my eyes, there was a shape kneeling in a front pew. Thick shoulders and a shadowy head lifted, staring up at the dark cross. I shook the sleep from my brain, looked again.

The figure stood up, a squat old man. Heavy hands held a wood rosary. The face was old, the square jaw had a long scar to the temple, there was a sunken hole in the cheek. He walked with a rolling gait to the flickering row of candles. He lit a candle, stared down at it, then set it on the rack.

"Stanic?" I said, "Josef Stanic?"

I saw him stiffen. That was all – stiffen. He stood motionless before the flickering candles. Then he turned on his heel and rushed out a side door.

*   *   *

"Find my grandfather, Mr. Fortune," Kate Vytautis had said.

She was a big, handsome girl in faded blue jeans, a dark blue shirt full of high breasts, and a blue headband that held back dark blonde hair. In the SoHo loft she sat restless in a chair among the steel and stone of Pete Howell's sculptures.

"He's eighty," she said. "Maybe he's hurt, sick."

Until the fifties, SoHo – south of Houston Street – had been an old area of commercial lofts where the small sweatshop factories had exploited immigrant labor at the turn of the century. Then the artists moved in, wanting the cheap old lofts with their vast space for giant paintings and mammoth sculptures. Illegal lofts then, not zoned for living, the artists hiding their children.

"He's just gone, Mr. Fortune," the girl said. Her face was serious, almost motherly, when she spoke of her grandfather, yet she squirmed like a half-grown Great Dane.

"Where did you see him last?" I asked.

"At his room up in Yorkville. Saturday morning."

"He lives alone?'

She nodded. "Grandmother Stanic died before I was born, soon after they came from Yugoslavia. He likes the old area."

"You're Yugoslavs?"

"We're Lithuanian."

American speech and manner, but raised in the more rigid culture of Old Country parents.

"What made you first decide he was missing?" I said.

"We have a big family dinner out at Springs every April eighteenth. A Commemoration. My father's sister and mother were taken away by the Germans in Lithuania on April eighteenth, 1943. They never came back. The young men were in the forests then, my father couldn't help. The dinner is very important to everyone, especially to my grandfather. Very, very important."

"And he didn't show up?"

"No." She got up, began to walk around among Pete's massive sculptures in the shadows of the loft. "I called him in the afternoon. He doesn't have a phone in his room, the landlady calls him to the phone. He wasn't there. Mother and I got worried, so I came back to town Sunday, went to his room. At his age you worry he could be dead inside if there's no answer, so I got the landlady to open his door. He wasn't there. On Sundays he sleeps late, but yesterday his bed was all made up."

"Maybe he's angry at your parents? Stayed away for that?"

"My father and he don't get along, but that's never kept him away – he wouldn't let it." The girl chewed on her thumb, a childish reflex. "He doesn't have many friends any more. I talked to all of them Sunday, and no one had seen him since early Saturday. He usually eats at the Dubrovnik on Eighty-fourth Street, but he hasn't been there all weekend. When he still wasn't at his room this morning, I checked where he works. He wasn't there either. He hadn't called in sick or anything. He just didn't show up."

"Dan?" Pete said. "I'll pay your fee."

What could I say? She cared for the old man, she was worried, it was my work. "I get a hundred a day now, Pete," I said. "Give me fifty, and I'll see if I can find him. I'll need his address, the names of his friends, the places he goes, and a description."

Kate Vytautis smiled. If she'd given me that smile earlier, I'd have said yes sooner. A marvelous smile, young and bright. An American girl, and yet different. Both more mature and less sophisticated at the same time. She began talking, giving me the information I'd asked for, and I got it all in my notebook.

Then she showed me a photo. No taller than his granddaughter, Josef Stanic was twice as wide as the girl. Half turned in the snapshot, he glared at the camera as if startled, suspicious at being photographed. A strong, rectangular face with none of the Oriental cast of many Russians and Bulgars – a South Slav. It was a weathered, lined face full of seams and hollows, with deep-set eyes. One of the hollows was a sunken hole in his cheek that looked like an old bullet wound. He had a long scar on the left from jaw to temple. His thick hair was almost white, and his eyes were as blue as his granddaughter's.

I left them in the loft, Kate Vytautis staring into space, Pete Howell staring at Kate. She was probably thinking about old Josef Stanic, Pete wasn't. He had it bad for the girl.

I took the subway up to Yorkville and walked to Josef Stanic's address. The noise of the crowds in the beer halls drifted down from Eighty-sixth Street. He lived in a well-kept rooming house with scrubbed steps and clean windows. The landlady acted like a concierge, small and brisk, but Berlin not Paris.

"Old Josef?" she said. "No, he has not returned. You are police?"

"Private. His granddaughter Kate hired me."

"Then you must see his room," she said crisply.

It was on the third floor. A combination bedroom-living room, the bed covered with a throw to serve as a couch. I made a quick search, but there was nothing – no papers, letters, or even an address book.

"I have not seen him since Saturday, about four P.M., on his way out." She watched me. "But he has his own keys, is a quiet man. I do not spy on my tenants."

"What was he like when he left?"

She thought. "He had his rosary when he went out. I saw him put it into his pocket. A large wooden rosary, hand-carved, and it was not a holy day or the anniversary of his wife's death. His church is on First Avenue. Saint Stanislaus."

I went back out to the street. It had started to rain. I got dimes in a bar, checked out the hospitals, the police, and the morgue. No Josef Stanic. So far, so good.

At Saint Stanislaus, Father Anton Kreska wore the old-fashioned black soutane. He had not seen Josef Stanic. "Not even on Sunday. Is something wrong?"

"I was going to ask you," I said.

"He did miss mass on Sunday."

"But he came to church Saturday evening?"

"No. I have not seen Josef since Sunday week."

Call it a hunch. A man who takes his rosary intends to go to church at some point, probably sooner than later. A religious man who had missed Sunday mass, and who wasn't dead, arrested, or in a hospital.

I waited three hours. Then Josef Stanic came to Saint Stanislaus.

■ ■ ■

I stood on the deserted Yorkville side street in the slackening drizzle, looking all around. Stanic had vanished. Fast and neat. Some old man. Had Kate Vytautis forgotten to tell me something? One thing was sure – Josef Stanic didn't want to be found, at least not by a stranger.

Meet the Author:
Dennis Lynds

A raconteur and Renaissance man, Dennis Lynds changed the mystery form and along the way created colorful private detectives who consistently won awards as well as the hearts of readers. He was a tall, lanky man with a nose the size of Gibraltar and a generous nature that made him a soft touch for friends, panhandlers, and his children. He published some 40 novels under various pseudonyms, won awards such as the Edgar, the mystery world's highest honor, and received accolades from legendary authors like Ross Macdonald. "A novelist of power and quality, ... one of the major imaginative creators in the crime field," Macdonald wrote of him.

The New York Times named several of Lynds's novels to its Best Mysteries of the Year lists. Remarkably, two of them written under different pseudonyms appeared on the same list – *Silent Scream* by Michael Collins and *Circle of Fire* by Mark Sadler.

Amused, Lynds said that none of the *Times* editors realized he was both Collins and Sadler. "I don't think they ever figured it out," he explained. And he never bothered to tell them.

Seldom does an author change the course of a genre once; rarely twice. Lynds is credited with being the writer who, in the late 1960s and early 1970s, propelled the detective novel into the Modern Age. His most famous pen name was Michael Collins. With that name, he created the opinionated Dan Fortune, the star of one of America's longest-running private detective series. The first book, *Act of Fear*, won the Edgar Allan Poe Award for Best First Novel. "Many critics believe Dan Fortune to be the culmination of a maturing process that transformed the private eye from the naturalistic Spade (Dashiell

Hammett) through the romantic Marlowe (Raymond Chandler) and the psychological Archer (Ross Macdonald) to the sociological Fortune," according to *Private Eyes: 101 Knights* by Robert Baker and Michael Nietzel.

At heart, Lynds was a rebel. Two decades later, he rattled mystery critics and changed the field again, this time by introducing literary techniques into the genre, beginning in the late 1980s with *Red Rosa, Castrato*, and *Chasing Eights*, and continuing well into the 1990s with *The Irishman's Horse, Cassandra in Red*, and *The Cadillac Cowboy*. Other authors followed, proving the flexibility and durability of the suspense world. "No one could accuse [Lynds] of reworking the same turf in his novels. . . . His last several books have pushed the private-eye form into some fascinating new shapes," according to *The Wall Street Journal* in 2000. *The Los Angeles Times* commented, "It takes style to bring that off. Bravery, too, of course."

Lynds also published mainstream novels, short stories, and poetry. Five of his literary short stories were honored in *Best American Short Stories*.

During World War II, he was a rifleman and carried books of poetry in his knapsack as he fought across France. He was a strong swimmer, so when he and fellow infantrymen were surrounded by Nazis, he plunged into an icy river, leading them to escape. He earned two Purple Hearts and a Bronze Star. Later he graduated with a degree in chemistry from Hofstra and a masters degree in journalism from Syracuse. A lifelong New Yorker, in the mid 1960s he finally left the East Coast's bitter winters to settle in the warm sunshine of Southern California. He was married three times, to Doris Flood, then Sheila McErlean, and finally to Gayle Hallenbeck Stone Lynds. He had two daughters, Katie and Deirdre Lynds, and two step children, Paul and Julia Stone.

Dennis Lynds died at age 81 in 2005. Jack Adrian wrote in *The Financial Times*, "Unusually for a mystery writer – as a breed, they tend to favor things as they are, rather than as they might be – the American author Dennis Lynds, politically, came from left of center.

This did not mean he preached bloody revolution. He wrote to entertain." Entertainment was something Lynds never forgot, that and to be generous to his friends.

Obituaries celebrating his work appeared around the globe. In a typical understatement, he commented near the end of his life, "I had a good run." His career had lasted more than fifty years.

Blue Death
#7 in the Edgar Award–winning Dan Fortune mystery series
by Dennis Lynds
Originally published under the pseudonym Michael Collins

Dan Fortune, the iconic private detective who operates out of New York's bohemian Chelsea district, has just taken on a baffling case. It should've been an ordinary business transaction, but Leslie Carter – Fortune's friend and a retired belly dancer – asks for help. It's time for her new husband to pay the lease on a parking garage they own, but her husband can't find anyone to take the money. A mammoth corporation has bought the property, and no one there will see him or talk with him about it. It's 1975, and the country is sliding toward recession. Already on a financial cliff, the Carters will lose everything if they can't hold onto the lease.

When Fortune goes out to handle the matter, he finds himself the victim of a strange runaround, too. But his ends in murder.

From Manhattan's executive towers to the raucous saloons and bordellos of Hoboken, Fortune is caught up in the lives of men so powerful they can order murder with a nod, and of twisted criminals who openly attack him to stop his probing. There are women, too, some greedy, some gentle, who conceal private nightmares behind smooth smiles.

Someone is hiding the secret that has driven an unlikely killer to murder, and no matter what, Fortune intends to uncover him – or her.

"A gripping story." – *The Charlotte Observer*

"A master of crime fiction." – *Ellery Queen Mystery Magazine*

"He is an admirable stylist, a master of mood and effect." – *New York Times*

A "satisfyingly intricate mystery. . . . Action and intrigue are nicely mixed." – *Publishers Weekly*

###

www.ingramcontent.com/pod-product-compliance
Lightning Source LLC
Chambersburg PA
CBHW061232170626
46809CB00007B/2636